# MURDER OF A SCOUNDREL

*Gripping crime mystery fiction from the Welsh valleys*


PIPPA McCATHIE

& NICOLA CLIFFORD

Published by The Book Folks

London, 2024





ISBN 978-1-80462-267-4

www.thebookfolks.com

*In memory of the author, Pippa McCathie,
who passed away peacefully in April 2023.*

Murder of a Scoundrel was unfinished by Pippa McCathie before her sad passing in 2023. It has been carefully and skilfully completed by author Nicola Clifford, who worked diligently with Pippa's draft, and copious notes, to produce the version before you.

This book is the sixth standalone title in a series of murder mysteries set in Wales by Pippa McCathie. The full list of books, in order of publication, is as follows:

Murder in the Valleys
Murder at the Old Abbey
Murder by the River Usk
Murder in a Welsh Town
Murder of a Gentleman
Murder of a Scoundrel

Full details can be found at the back of this book.

You don't have to read these other books to enjoy this one, but we're sure you'll love it so much that you will afterwards.

# Prologue

They'd hidden their bikes behind some brambles near the entrance to the disused tunnel, just in case someone came along and interrupted their adventure.

"Come on. There's some sort of barrier a bit further on but we can climb over it, easy." The older boy always took the lead.

"I don't know. My mam would kill us if she knew we'd come here. She says it's not safe; bricks and stuff fall–"

"Mammy's boy, mammy's boy! Must do as he's told!" the older boy chanted.

The scorn burnt. He straightened his back. "Okay then, let's go."

Pushing aside some vines that hung over the entrance to the Usk railway tunnel, they crunched their way slowly along in the gloom. The floor was a mess of gravel, fallen bits of masonry, weeds and dead leaves blown in over time. Here and there were pools of dirty water. Moss-covered bricks curved above them and, as they got further in, the sun faded, apart from the odd patch coming from shafts in the roof. No weeds grew in the darkness. It became colder. The older boy held up his phone, using it as a torch. It lit up the interior, making it seem even more eerie. Soon they came to metal railings that barred their way, but a quick squeeze round and they were both on the other side.

After a minute, the younger boy whispered, "I don't think we should go any further. Come on, let's go back."

"Don't be so wet. We might find something interesting. You never know. My mam told me a king slept here once when his train stopped for the night."

"A king?"

"Yeah, and I looked it up and it was someone called Edward the eighth. Can't remember when it was, probably hundreds of years ago. He abju– abdi– abdocated, whatever that means. Perhaps it's like decapitated, maybe they cut off his head and his ghost haunts the tunnel – woo, woo, woo." He laughed at his companion's reaction. "You should see your face, mush. Scaredy cat!"

A scuttling sound brought him up short.

"What was that?" the younger boy exclaimed, and his voice echoed round the bricks overhead.

The older boy, a little less sure of himself now, pointed a bit further in. "See that hollow bit? It's what's called a recess and I'll tell you for why. It was for people to get out of the way when a train came along. We can hide in there."

He stomped ahead and, afraid to be left behind, the other quickly followed in his footsteps, cannoning into him when he suddenly stopped.

"What's that over there?" the older boy asked.

"Where?"

"There." He pointed the light on his phone into the brick-lined alcove.

It was a couple of metres high and about a metre deep. Three rows of russet-red bricks, neatly placed, curved over the top. To one side lay what looked like a pile of clothes, but from under them a leg poked out, pale skin showing above a sock and a man's shoe.

"Shit, shit, shit," said the younger boy. "Is he asleep or what?"

They both crept forward, but the figure didn't stir. Surely, he had heard them talking, or heard their feet crunching on the gravel.

"Mister!" the older boy said. His voice shook a little as he spoke. "Mister?"

He darted forward, hand outstretched, and grabbed at the dark coat. It fell away to reveal a pale damp face, one eye half open and sightless, the other nothing but a mass of blood and bone where the skull had caved in.

Both boys stood, transfixed, as the seconds ticked by. Then, without a word, they turned and ran back along the tunnel, the sound of their feet echoing around them. Gasping for breath, they squeezed past the barrier. A moment later, they grabbed their bikes and cycled back along the way they'd come, as if there were ghosts on their heels.

# Chapter 1

Fabia Havard had taken a break from the illustrations she'd been commissioned to draw. She'd wrapped her daughter, Bethan, up warm in her buggy and gone for a walk through Gwiddon Park with her close friend Cath Temple, vicar of St Cybi's Church in Pontygwyn. They were now sitting either side of Fabia's kitchen table clasping mugs of hot coffee in an effort to warm up. The late February day was chilly, and the wind had been brisk. Bethan was fast asleep, and Fabia was hoping she'd stay that way. She wanted to hear more from Cath.

What she'd heard so far had worried her deeply, particularly because Cath seemed to be treating the matter as if it were a common problem in her line of work. It may well be, but that didn't make Fabia feel any better.

"Cath, you've mentioned this bloke before," Fabia began, wondering how to express what she was thinking without sounding overdramatic. "If he… sorry, what did you say his name was?"

"Huw Prosser, he's a sidesman at church."

"Oh Lord. I think I've met him, haven't I? He's the short chap who wears those red trousers, a blazer and a cravat? And he's got that ridiculous curly moustache. He's really smarmy. That one time I met him, I thought I recognised him, but it's probably just that he's a particular type, you know – short, balding, blustery. I can't believe he tried it on with you."

Cath smiled at Fabia's description. "Yes, it was rather awkward, but I think I managed to put him off."

"If he's getting to be a nuisance," Fabia said, "don't you think you should do something about it before it gets out of hand?"

"Other than that one time, all he's done is be overly helpful. He keeps saying that his experience in the army means he's good at organising things. Oh, and he did ask me out for a drink."

"Did you go?"

"No, not yet," Cath said. "He's asked me several times, sometimes to his house and sometimes to the pub, so he probably will again."

"What you describe is a bit more than just being helpful," Fabia pointed out. "Phoning you nearly every day and interrupting your conversations with others. Does any other single male parishioner pop round to the vicarage with flowers on a regular basis? Don't forget that time he came around late in the evening, that's a bit weird."

"He said that was because it was a time when he knew he'd catch me at home." Cath wasn't sounding quite so casual about it now. "I suppose he is a bit of a pain, but I can deal with it."

"Are you sure?" Fabia frowned across at her friend. "Don't leave it too long before you tell him to get lost."

"I can't really do that, can I? He's one of my parishioners and I have a duty of care to all of them."

Fabia gave an exasperated sigh. "That doesn't mean you have to put up with him badgering you."

"No, but I do have to tread carefully, Fabia. I thought you'd understand." Cath sounded rather put out by Fabia's reaction.

Fabia leant across the table and clasped Cath's hand. "I do, it's just that I worry about you. I know! You should invent a boyfriend, someone who works abroad or on ships or something."

Her friend grinned a little sheepishly. "Well, I have investigated one of those websites, you know, the ones that promise to find you the man of your dreams."

Fabia raised her eyebrows.

"You suggested it a while ago, and I thought, well, why not?" Cath said.

"That's exciting," Fabia said.

"One of the women in the choir, Jo Bedward, was talking about finding a boyfriend – well, a manfriend – online. So I had a look myself."

"And?" asked Fabia. "Have you found anyone interesting?"

Cath's cheeks reddened a little. "I have made friends with one nice bloke; just talking online, nothing more."

"That's great, Cath," Fabia said. "But what would the bishop say if he knew you were considering online dating?"

"I'm not going to think about that. Anyway, I'm not about to tell him."

"Cath!" Fabia smiled at her friend who grinned back. "Just promise me you'll be careful, and be firm with this Huw character. You really don't want that situation to escalate."

"I suppose not. Maybe I'll have a word with the rural dean." She didn't sound particularly keen on the idea.

"Is he the appropriate person in the hierarchy?"

"Yes, he's in charge of pastoral care for the diocese."

"Do you get on well with him?"

"Enough. He's a bit of a dry old stick, but kind." Cath gave her a slightly twisted smile. "But it won't come to that. You worry too much."

"I have reason," Fabia said earnestly, "and I care about you."

"I know, love." Cath came around the table and gave Fabia a hug. "I'll be careful. Now I must get going." She leant down to look in the buggy and saw that Bethan was waking up. "Hallo, sweetheart, your mam's just here. Thanks for the coffee, Fabia. I'll let myself out."

When Cath had gone, Fabia reached into the buggy to lift Bethan out. "You know something," she told her daughter, "I'm going to have a nosey about this Huw chap. Perhaps I'll have a word with Geraldine, she goes to church regularly, so she'll probably know him. Better safe than sorry."

Bethan blew a bubble and Fabia took that as agreement.

# Chapter 2

Fabia's partner, Chief Inspector Matt Lambert, was having a boring day. He leant back in his chair and yawned, then closed his eyes. He snapped them open a moment later as he heard a knock at his office door. Sergeant Dilys Bevan came in, laptop in hand.

She grinned. "Bad night, sir?"

"Somewhat. Bethan's teeth are giving her jip, and I think she's getting a cold."

"Ah, poor pet."

"I suggested that if she didn't pick up this morning, Fabia should ring the doctor, but she told me not to fuss." He frowned across at Dilys. "I hope it's nothing worse."

"I'm sure it isn't," said Dilys, who had several nieces and nephews and was used to the ways of babies. "You worry too much."

"Probably. Okay, Dilys, what have you got for me?"

"It's this e-mail that's just come through from the NFIB – that's the National Fraud Intelligence Bureau. They're based with the City of London force, but I believe they cover…" Dilys paused when she saw the expression on her boss's face. "Sorry, of course you know all that.

Anyway, they've got a fraud case they think has connections to this area."

"What kind of fraud?"

"Looks like a mixture to me. Pulling people in who access a website looking for sex or romance, then offering them opportunities to make thousands if they invest in so-called business ventures, or going on about a sick relative who needs financial help and getting money out of them that way. Have a look." She put her laptop down on his desk and turned it towards him. She pointed to part of the e-mail. "This is the one they believe is based round here. They've identified the bloke in this photo as a Seth Geddings."

"How did they get the photo?"

"He was on record as having been arrested in Swansea for hacking into small businesses with a view to blackmail. The local police got as far as sending the case to the CPS, but it never came to trial. That was seven years ago. The photo would have been taken then. The date matched."

"And what now?"

"They've traced him to the Newport area, probably round Usk or Pontygwyn way. They say the amounts he's scammed out of people run into thousands, but that's par for the course."

Matt frowned at the photo of a fair-haired man with a thin face and eyes rather close together. "Does his name ring a bell with you?" he asked.

"Sorry, but no. I've got Claire Gooding conducting a search to see if he's known to us, but she's only just started."

"Okay. Send this through to me and I'll have a look. And tell Claire to bring me what she comes up with."

"Will do, sir," Dilys said. She glanced at her watch. "It's nearly half five. Why don't you go home early for once, see how your little one is doing?"

Matt stretched his long body back in his chair, then got up. "I think I will. It has been pretty quiet, hasn't it? Best take advantage of it while it lasts. I've just had a text from Fabia asking when I'll be home. She doesn't do that unless she has something on her mind."

Matt got up and shrugged on his coat, pushed a hand through his untidy hair, and grinned at Dilys. "If the truth were known, I miss the little monster even if she is keeping us awake all night. She's normally such an easy-going kid."

"And absolutely adorable with those reddish gold curls like her mother's. Go on, get home and give her a *cwtch*."

"Who? Fabia?"

"Both," Dilys said with a grin.

* * *

When Matt arrived home, Fabia was busy feeding Bethan, who was sitting in her high chair, banging a spoon on the tray, her face covered in the remains of her supper. When she saw Matt, she gave him a broad smile and said, "Da, da, da."

"Hallo, little one," Matt said, kissing the top of her head. "She looks more cheerful than she did this morning."

"She's fine," Fabia assured him. "You're just in time to bathe her and give her a bottle while I get the dinner ready."

Matt scooped up his daughter and took her upstairs. Fabia prepared Bethan's milk then started to chop onions for a shepherd's pie.

It wasn't until Bethan was asleep and they sat down to their meal that Fabia told Matt what was on her mind.

"Cath came around this morning. I'm rather worried about her."

"Why is that?"

Fabia told him about Huw Prosser pestering Cath. "She's being far too patient with him. If she isn't more assertive, he's going to take it as encouragement. The good news is she took my advice about going on one of these dating websites. She's often said – well, a few times – that she envies what we've got; our relationship, and Bethan and all."

"Does she?" Matt said. "I didn't know that."

"Well, maybe she's lonely. However many friends she has, in her position she has to be careful and not get too close to people."

"But she's close to you."

"I know, but I don't go to church that often," Fabia said, pushing her plate away. "She said one of her choir members has hooked up with someone she met online and Cath decided to check it out for herself."

"Is it okay for vicars to do that?" Matt asked, frowning. Then he grinned. "The thought of my father, or my brother, Piers, getting involved with a dating site is laughable."

Fabia grinned back then shrugged. "I don't know. Cath said she's not going to tell the bishop. She says she's met what she called a 'nice bloke'. She went quite pink when she mentioned him. It'll be really nice if she has someone special in her life. She deserves to be happy."

Matt looked across the table at Fabia, frowning. That report from the NFIB chimed all too clearly with what Fabia had told him. Of course, these people could be anywhere – London, Durham, Ghana, Malaysia – there were no boundaries in this age of social media and the internet. But it niggled at him. Dilys had said that the NFIB had mentioned a romance scam.

"Matt? What are you thinking?"

"It could be just a coincidence, but we had some info through from the NFIB this afternoon. There's a scammer they're interested in and they've worked out that he – or she – is working from this area."

Fabia shrugged. "What does that have to do with Cath?" Then her face fell. "Are you saying Cath could be being scammed with this dating website? Surely that's too much of a coincidence. These people could be anywhere in the world."

"True, but if this person wants to target someone they know, or someone that they've got a grudge against, for instance, it may be a case of hiding in plain sight."

"But why should they have a grudge against Cath?" Fabia asked.

"I've no idea, Fabia. Maybe she's offended someone with one of her sermons or got on the wrong side of a parishioner."

Fabia's eyes widened. "Now, that's a possibility. This Huw Prosser thinks he's God's gift. She says he's always trying to tell her how to do her job, talks about women as if they're a lesser breed, you know, the little-man syndrome. He made a pass–"

"Do people still do that?" Matt interrupted.

"You know what I mean," Fabia said, "and she had to be pretty firm about not being interested in having a relationship. I wonder…"

"You wonder what?" Matt asked when Fabia didn't go on.

"If he could be one of these scammers."

Matt gave a snort of laughter. "Come on, Fabia, that's a bit of a leap. Anyway, it doesn't seem very likely. I think I know who you mean. Isn't he in his fifties? But I suppose that's ageist."

"I suppose," Fabia said. "I might do a little probing when I next see Cath. I really don't want her taken for a ride, poor love. She has enough on her plate with the archdeacon being such an awkward bastard and the Mother's Union getting chopsy."

"You should hear my brother on the subject. My sister-in-law says some of the women in his parish compete for his attention as if she didn't even exist. What is it about a uniform, even if the uniform is a cassock?"

Fabia grinned at him. "Are you getting trouble from nubile young recruits, then?"

"Nah, I rarely wear a uniform and I talk far too much about you and Bethan." Matt put his hand out and pulled her to her feet. "Come on, my love, let's get this lot cleared up and go to bed. It'd be good to get some shut-eye before madam starts demanding attention at some ungodly hour."

# Chapter 3

"I should never have said it's been quiet," Matt said to Dilys the next morning.

"Asking for trouble, that is," Dilys told him, grinning.

"No need to rub it in," Matt growled. "Okay, run it past me again."

"We've got a knifing in Shaftesbury Park, the victim is alive but in intensive care; no one arrested as yet, usual searches are being done. We also have a break-in at that church on Queen's Hill – Inspector Evans is dealing with that. And then there's this Mrs Jameson who's brought in a couple of lads. Round about twelve or thirteen, they are, and she's asked for you by name."

"Has she now? Did she say why?"

"No, she didn't, but she says it's serious, and Karim Singh, who's on the reception desk, says the two boys look shit scared – whether of her or for some other reason, I don't know. One of them is her son, Aled, and the other a nephew called Cai Roberts. Karim says she's a pretty formidable woman."

"Why didn't she phone instead of bringing them in?" Matt demanded, irritated.

"She says she wanted to make sure she saw you and no one else. She wants to tell you the whole story. Karim has put them in interview room two."

Matt pushed himself out of his chair. "The name Jameson rings a bell, but I'm not sure why. Okay, let's go and see what they have to say for themselves."

The two of them made their way down the stairs to one of the interview rooms on the ground floor. Matt opened the door and they went in. There was a window on the right, set high in the wall, which looked out on an alleyway that ran down the back of the station building. The room would have been rather gloomy but for a florescent light that glared from the ceiling. The walls were a dull grey-blue and there was a large map of the Newport area on one and a framed photograph of the Steel Wave sculpture on another. At one end of a table jutting out from the left-hand wall was some standard-issue recording equipment, flanked by several padded office chairs.

As they entered, all three people sitting to one side of the table turned to look at them. In the centre was a woman who appeared to be in her thirties. Her bright orange hair was cropped shorter on one side of her head than the other, and her vivid-pink jumper made quite a contrast in colour. The boys sat either side of her; one had a shock of blond hair which looked as if it had little recent contact with a brush or comb, the other was darker with his hair shaved close at the sides. Both looked pale and scared.

Matt and Dilys sat down opposite them and introduced themselves, then Matt looked across at the woman. She seemed familiar.

"I believe we've met before," he said.

"We have. Last year, it was, when you arrested my ex 'cos he beat me up. You did a tidy job there, putting him away."

"Ah yes, I remember."

"That's why I asked to speak to you."

"I see." With a smile of reassurance, Matt added, "My sergeant will set up the recording equipment."

The woman looked a little wary at this, but she didn't protest. Dilys gave the time and date and then asked them for their full names.

"I'm Chelsea Jameson and this one y'ere" – she indicated the younger boy – "is my boy, Aled, and this one is my sister's boy, Cai."

"Perhaps you could tell us why you brought the two of them in, Mrs Jameson," Matt said.

"Well, it's like this. They was mitching–"

Matt's raised eyebrows stopped her in her tracks.

"Bunking off school," Dilys said quietly.

Matt nodded his understanding. "Please go on, Mrs Jameson."

"Here's the thing, these two tearaways were up at the Usk railway tunnel. I've told them straight, I have," she said, giving her son a soft slap on the back of the head. He crouched lower in his chair. "I've told them not to go up there. It's dangerous, bricks falling, low lifes doing their druggy stuff, and God knows what else. And I was right." She nodded in satisfaction.

"In what way?" asked Matt.

She paused and put up a hand to her chest, eyes dramatically wide. She's enjoying this, Matt thought.

"These two found a body." Mrs Jameson lowered her voice on the last two words and put an arm round each boy. Heads bent, they wriggled half-heartedly.

Matt frowned then glanced quickly at Dilys. "A body? In the tunnel?"

"That's what they told me, although I had to screw it out of them. I could see they'd had a shock, like, and their clothes were ripped, so I persuaded them to tell me what happened."

Dilys leant her crossed arms on the table and looked at the younger boy, her voice sympathetic. "I know this must be difficult for you, but can you tell us exactly what you found, and how? It would be very helpful."

Seconds ticked by until Mrs Jameson said, "Come on, speak up."

It was the older boy who sat forward and answered the question. "I'd read about the tunnel and I thought there'd be no harm in having a look. We were a bit of the way in and there was a barrier" – he shrugged – "but we thought we'd have a look at the other side."

"That barrier's there for good reasons," Mrs Jameson snapped.

"I know that now, Auntie Chel, but we didn't go far. It was when we came to a sort of hollow in the wall, where people got out of the way if a train was coming." He sounded proud of his knowledge, but then sagged and added, "He was in there." The boy swallowed and gave his head a shake as if clearing his mind of an unpleasant image. "It was buzzing," he muttered, "really horrible."

Aled began to cry, and Mrs Jameson tightened her grip around his shoulders, then rummaged in a pocket and handed him a tissue.

"I realise this is upsetting," Matt said, "but I do need to know exactly what you found."

It took a while, but Matt and Dilys gradually got the information they needed out of the two boys. Dilys arranged for two cans of Coke to be brought in for them, and for formal statements to be taken.

* * *

Within half an hour of their return to his office, Matt had sent two officers from uniform to go up to the railway tunnel and find out if the boys were telling the truth. It wasn't long before they called in and confirmed that there was a body.

"Looks as if he's been dead a while, sir," the senior of the two officers told Matt. "I'd estimate his age at about mid to late forties. Looks like someone hit him several times, the whole of the right side of his face has been bashed in. How on earth anyone managed to move a dead body such a distance is anyone's guess."

"Okay, I'll get the ball rolling. You and Craig stay and keep an eye," Matt said, then hang up.

"That certainly qualifies as throwing PC Craig Evans in at the deep end, sir," Dilys remarked.

"It does, but I had a reason for sending him. While he was doing his gardening jobs, he had another job conducting guided walks of the tunnel and the railway bridge. It might be useful that he knows the terrain. Another plus is that he's got a photographic memory."

"I didn't know that," Dilys said. "He's shaping up well, isn't he?"

"Yes, he is. Fabia said she thought he'd make a good officer. That was after Geraint Denbigh was killed. She was one of Craig's referees when he applied to join the force."

"He's a good lad."

"He is. Four years ago, I might not have said so, but I've changed my mind." Matt pushed himself out of his chair. "Right, let's get on with it."

* * *

A couple of hours later, Matt and Dilys parked as near as they could to the vine-strewn entrance of the railway tunnel. There were several other vehicles already there: a police car, the SOCOs' dark vans and another civilian car which they recognised as belonging to Dr Pat Curtis, the local police surgeon. There was the usual blue and white crime scene tape flapping in a brisk breeze, barring the way to any intruders. Matt noticed that there were no ghouls, as he called them, standing around gawping. The news obviously hadn't filtered out yet.

At this time of year, it was an eerie place, full of shadows among the out-of-control brambles. As they walked along the path towards the arched entrance, Dilys, hands deep in her coat pockets, said, "I don't mind telling you, this would not be my choice for an afternoon walk."

"I don't know. I dare say it's quite interesting. Plenty of history if you do the whole walk from Usk town centre past the castle," Matt said, not being of a fanciful frame of mind. Facts, that's what he believed in, facts. Although those who thought he lacked imagination were wrong. He just insisted that facts were what he cared about, not fanciful theories.

Craig Evans was standing at the entrance. Dilys noticed that he looked a little pale. "You okay, constable?" she asked.

He nodded his head but didn't elaborate.

"The SOCOs are all by there," he told them, pointing down the tunnel, "and Dr Curtis has just arrived."

"Ah, I wonder what mood she's in," Matt said.

"She's not that bad," Dilys said.

Matt quirked an eyebrow at her but didn't comment. "How long have they been here?" he asked Craig.

"About an hour, I'd say."

"That's just the beginning, it'll take days yet."

Craig nodded.

At that moment, an older constable trudged out of the tunnel entrance, pulling back the hood of his white suit as he came. "Good morning, Sarge," he said. "I thought you might be here about now. Karen Johns is in charge of the team. She said to ask you to come right in when you arrived."

Matt had encountered Karen Johns before. She was a talented and efficient forensics expert. He was glad she was heading up the team.

"Will do. Let's have the kit, Dilys."

Dilys shrugged a backpack off her shoulders and unzipped it. Soon, she and Matt were kitted out in white suits and face masks.

They began their walk down the shadowy tunnel. It smelt of dead leaves, damp, and old bricks, and they could hear the drip, drip of water from somewhere further in. It was cold and clammy, the floor uneven in places, and Matt found it doubly unpleasant in this weather. Maybe it would be more welcoming in mid-summer, and definitely less cold. They came to a barrier of metal railings which had been pushed aside. Behind it, they could see the forensics team hard at work in their regulation white PPE suits. It gave them a ghostly look in the bright light of the halogen lamps that had been rigged up.

A tall woman in a similar suit came towards them as they approached. "Chief Inspector, good, I'm glad you're here."

"What have we got, Karen?" Matt asked.

"A male, late forties I'd say. I don't think he was killed here. He must have been brought here and dumped. I gather there was maintenance going on up until last Thursday, that's five days ago, so he was probably brought here between then and last night. He was killed by heavy blows to the right side of the head. There may be other injuries, but we haven't moved the body yet. Dr Curtis is having a preliminary look and, as usual" – she smiled ruefully at Matt – "she says we'll have to be patient. She pointed out that she's not a miracle worker."

Matt returned the smile. "Anything to identify him?"

"No, nothing in his pockets; no mobile phone, wallet, nothing; nor any signs of how he was brought here. It's a long way to the entrance."

"Oh great!" Matt muttered. "Thanks, Karen. I'll go and have a quick word with the doctor."

Steeling himself, Matt walked towards the group of people gathered round the entrance to a recess in the curving tunnel. However many dead bodies he'd had to look at, he never quite got used to it. Fabia told him he probably never would, and he shouldn't expect to. He supposed she was right.

Pat Curtis's slim figure was bending over the body. She looked up as Matt approached, gave him a curt nod and stood up.

"Good afternoon, Doctor. What have you found so far?" Matt asked.

"Not a lot. As you can probably see, the head injury certainly did it for him. I'll know more when I get him back to the lab."

Matt turned to Karen. "Can he be moved yet?"

"Yes. We'll be here a while, seeing if we can find anything else, but as the doctor says, she can't really do much more here."

Matt nodded. "Right. Better get him out then."

Two of the SOCO team brought up a stretcher and body bag and they manoeuvred the dead man into it and began to carry him slowly out to one of the vans.

"Any idea when he was killed, Doctor?" Matt asked.

"No. Rigor has passed and he's into secondary flaccidity. It's pretty cold in here so that would have to be taken into account. I'd say days rather than hours, that's for sure. I'll have more for you once I've had time to do a proper examination. I am fairly sure he wasn't killed here, though. There's nowhere near enough blood considering the severity of the injury."

Matt watched as she turned to follow the stretcher out of the tunnel, then she turned back. "One slightly unusual thing I noticed might be helpful to you – the middle fingers on his right hand have been broken, as if they'd been bent right back until they dislocated and then snapped."

He heard Dilys mutter something to herself. When he glanced at her, she shook her head.

"Nasty," Matt said. "Well, thank you, Doctor." He knew, from experience, that he would get no more out of her at this stage. He'd just have to be patient.

As he and Dilys made their way back to their car, he asked, "Did the broken fingers mean anything to you?"

"No, not really, at least not immediately. It was a sort of feeling of déjà vu, but I can't pin it down."

"Let me know if you remember what it reminded you of."

"Will do, sir, it's really bugging me," Dilys said.

* * *

Later that afternoon, as Matt walked through the main office on his way back from getting a coffee from the machine, Dilys called out, "Sir, there's another case come in."

"What kind of case?" he asked wearily. "Another body?"

"No. This time it's a missing person. It's come from the South Wales force in Bridgend, circulated all over as usual. A male, forty-five, name of Jake Seddon, reported missing three days ago by his wife who says he went to Cardiff last week on business, but he hasn't come home. She was expecting him back on the same day… Saturday."

"Any more info about him?"

"She says he's a pharmacist. The reason I picked up on it was this photo of him." Dilys indicated an image on the screen of her laptop. "Does that remind you of someone, sir?"

Matt frowned at the photo of a man with a shaved head wearing wire-rimmed glasses. The most distinctive things about him were his flattened boxer's nose and a patch of darker skin on his left cheek.

Matt pointed to this. "What's that called?"

"Hyperpigmentation," Dilys said. "Compare it to this photo of the bloke who was found in the tunnel."

For a moment or two, Matt stood looking from one photo to the other. In spite of the injury to the dead man's face, it clearly showed the shape of his nose and the different colouring of the skin, and they both matched up with the photo of the missing man.

"Well done, Dilys. I think you've got something here. Get on to Bridgend and see if you can find out more about the bloke who's missing."

* * *

A while later, Dilys came into Matt's office looking pleased with herself. "Right, sir, here's the latest. I spoke to an Inspector Kapoor in Bridgend. I e-mailed the photos taken at the scene and he agrees that it looks like the same man. He says they've found out a bit more about him. You know his wife said he was a pharmacist? Well, it seems Bridgend suspect that he's involved with a gang selling unlicensed drugs and think he's in charge of manufacturing. It's a pretty lucrative trade, as we know only too well."

"But they haven't been able to prove this man is involved?"

"That's about it. Inspector Kapoor says they searched the house but found no evidence on the premises. They still haven't managed to find out where his laboratory is. He's going to speak to Mrs Seddon – Gwyneth, her name is – and show her the photo of the dead man to see if she can identify him."

Matt frowned, thinking how traumatic that would be for the poor woman, but these things had to be done. He nodded to Dilys. "Get back to him and tell him yes, and to let us know if she confirms it's her husband."

"I'll get onto that right now," Dilys said.

"I've got to go upstairs and report to the boss," Matt told her, "then, after that, I hope to go home, but I'll come and check with you before leaving."

"Rightio, sir."

# Chapter 4

Chief Superintendent Erica Talbot had been in post for nearly a year now and Matt still marvelled at the difference it had made to his job, and to the team's work generally. Her predecessor, Charlie Rees-Jones, had been a traditionalist who hated to rock any boats. If any case involved one of his high-profile friends, particularly those from his masonic lodge, Matt had not been allowed a free hand. He'd felt as if it wasn't just the criminals getting in his way but Rees-Jones too. Erica Talbot was no soft touch, but she was approachable and pragmatic. Matt thoroughly enjoyed working with her, except for one thing.

Several months ago, before Bethan was born, and not long after Erica Talbot had taken up her new post, she'd spoken to Fabia about returning to the Gwent force. She'd said she wanted to offer further training to the local multi-agency safeguarding hub, known as the Local Safeguarding Children's Board, and that it would be a civilian post.

Matt hadn't been too keen, but wasn't entirely sure why. It wasn't just the problems of finding a child-minder for Bethan. There was more to it than that. Resolutely he'd pushed the niggling worries to the back of his mind, but now they'd returned as Fabia had her first meeting with the team tomorrow. He was feeling exasperated with himself, and with Fabia, as he knocked at the chief's door.

Small and slim, her short hair greying and her eyes sharply blue behind her glasses, Erica Talbot looked up as Matt came in. She could be formidable when angry or dissatisfied, and at first Matt had found her hard to suss out. She'd seemed sort of closed-in, but he'd discovered that she could also be kind and perceptive, and that she had a dry sense of humour.

She looked up and smiled as he came in. "Ah, Chief Inspector, have you got any news for me?"

"Some, ma'am, but not as much as I'd like."

"Take a seat," she said.

Matt did so and began his report. She listened in silence, concentrating on his every word and asking the occasional question.

Once he'd finished, she said, "It seems to me you're doing everything you can," then changed the subject. "I'm really looking forward to seeing Fabia tomorrow at the LSCB meeting. She's just the right person to pull them together into a more useful unit."

"I'm sure she will," Matt said, his voice a little constrained.

Ever direct, his boss asked, "Are you unhappy with the idea of her coming back?"

"No, no – I'm sure she'll do a great job."

"But…?"

"Perhaps it's just that I worry about the effect it will have on her. Her retirement didn't actually go very smoothly and she has several commissions to work on, and of course we have Bethan now. I'm just, well, worried it could be too much for her."

"I think that you're just going to have to trust her. I'm sure she'll be fine." She smiled across at him. "We women are a good deal tougher than some men may think."

Matt nodded, his answering smile a little strained. "That's more or less what Fabia has said."

"A woman after my own heart," Erica Talbot said, then she rose from her chair. "I must get going. I have a meeting that I'd much rather duck, but needs must. Keep me posted on your progress on the Seddon case, and the other two cases as well."

Matt rose too and opened the door for her. "I will, ma'am."

They walked down the passage to the stairs together and Matt was pleased that the subject of Fabia's new job was not brought up again.

* * *

On Thursday morning, Fabia left the house feeling a little nervous.

"It's all a bit fragmented at the moment," Erica had told her, "and obviously underfunded as always. Although all the different stakeholders do a good job, it occurred to me that it would help them if someone was in post to oversee and co-ordinate. A chairperson, a sort of umbrella. They're all overworked: teachers, GPs, paramedics, social workers, Citizens Advice and, of course, the police force."

Fabia had laughed. "I've never been likened to an umbrella before." But she'd understood what Erica meant. She'd been most intrigued by the idea, particularly as she'd been involved in setting up the LSCB group in Newport before she left the force. Back then, she'd worked closely with the director of children's services in the town and had come to admire her and her team, and the almost impossible job they had to do.

Matt seemed to be worried that it would be problematic if they were working together again. "After all," he'd said hesitantly, "the last time we worked together, well, it did go a bit pear-shaped, didn't it?"

"Through no fault of mine, Matt," Fabia had protested. "We worked together for years with no problems, until those bastards got the better of me and you buggered off.

But we sorted that out years ago," she added, not wanting to start an argument.

She suspected that, deep down, he was wary of her encroaching on his territory, although she was sure he would never admit it. He might not even be aware that he was. Both she and Erica had pointed out that they weren't likely to cross paths even if she did take the job, and she could easily fit it in round her work as an artist. As for Bethan, Fabia was close to organising care for her. Mrs Pritchard, who came in to do some cleaning each week, had a daughter who'd just registered as a child-minder. She'd said she'd have room for Bethan. When Fabia had a better idea of the hours she would be working, she'd set that up as well.

Now all the paperwork had been done, contracts signed, the different agencies consulted, and she was about to have her first meeting with the personnel involved. Today, she dropped Bethan off with Cath and made her way into Newport. As she'd parked her car and got out, she'd looked up at the building that had played such a big part in her life. She'd given a determined nod and thought, okay, here we go.

Fabia was shown up to the chief superintendent's office and Erica greeted her warmly, shook her by the hand and said, "Have a seat and let me bring you up to speed on the personnel. You're nice and early so we've got plenty of time."

"Being back here feels a little surreal," Fabia admitted.

Erica smiled. "I should imagine it does. How long exactly is it since you left?"

This was a question she could answer immediately, the date was engraved on her heart. "I started that euphemistic sick leave on 30th November 2016 and officially retired about eighteen months later."

"And thanks to Matt and Alun Richards–"

"And a few others," Fabia said.

"Indeed – thanks to them you were cleared of all involvement in the Cwmberis fraud. It must have undermined your confidence somewhat. Do you feel it did?"

Fabia sat up straighter in her chair. She said nothing for a moment, then gave a little nod. "Yes, I think it did, but I'm much better now than I was. The first case that Matt dealt with after we met up again was rather close to home. A young artist friend of mine was killed, and her murderer nearly did for me as well. That took some recovering from. I had nightmares for a while, but Matt and my close friends helped me through that. I'm back to my old self now," she added firmly.

"That's the impression I get," Erica said.

"Thank you." Fabia thought it was time they got down to work. "It seems that the same agencies are represented on the LSCB team as there were when I set it up. Could you give me a few tips on the current members? I know their names, but I'd like some idea of their ages and personalities, and attitudes, perhaps?"

"I've printed out a list for you." Erica passed a sheet of A4 across the desk. "I'll e-mail it to you as well, but I thought this would be useful. I always think it's a bit disconcerting if someone spends all their time looking at a screen rather than at the people in a meeting. Have a look through it."

Fabia scanned the list. There was a senior social worker representing the local children's services, a woman called Joanna Forrest. There was a probation officer called George Morris, whose name Fabia recognised; she remembered meeting him on several occasions before she retired, unfortunately it was not a positive memory. The manager of the local Citizens Advice, Rhiannon Haydon, was also a member, as was Chloe Daniels in her role as family liaison officer. A senior community nurse, Amelia Thomas, was also on the list. The name was vaguely familiar. The last name was a local GP, Dr Jay Anand.

Erica had waited quietly for her comments. As Fabia looked up, she asked, "What do you think?"

"This is pretty close to the group I set up all those years ago, although many of the personnel have changed. I do know one of them – George Morris – I'm not sure he'll be all that pleased to see me. We had a few run-ins back in the day."

"I'm sure you'll be able to handle him."

"I expect so. I also know Chloe Daniels, she's a very good officer. Amelia Thomas rings a bell, but I'm not sure why."

"Perhaps you came across her during your pregnancy," Erica suggested.

"That could be it."

"Well, shall we get going? I'll introduce you and then leave you to it."

Erica led her along a corridor and downstairs to the floor below. They came to a door marked 'Conference Room' and below that, 'meeting in progress'. Fabia could hear a murmur of voices but when they entered the room, the people sitting round an oval table fell silent. Fabia took a deep breath and put a smile on her face.

# Chapter 5

Later that day, Matt sat at his desk feeling frustrated. Inspector Kapoor hadn't yet come back to him to confirm the identification of the man found in the railway tunnel and there wasn't a lot they could do until he did. Pat Curtis had told him she hadn't completed the post-mortem yet, although she had conceded that she would try to get the results to him early in the afternoon. He sincerely hoped she would, as his hands were tied until he knew more about the victim. What was holding things up in Bridgend? Karen Johns hadn't been able to provide him with much either. In spite of a search of every inch of the tunnel and the surrounding woods, they'd found little that seemed to be of any significance.

He was about to go and get a cup of coffee from the machine when there was a knock on his office door. He looked around to see Fabia standing in the doorway.

"Fabia," Matt said, taken aback, "of course, you had that meeting today, didn't you?" he added, his tone a little cool.

Dilys followed her in. "Hiya, Fabia. Was it your first meeting with the LSCB team this morning?"

"Yes, it was," Fabia said, glancing at Matt. "I thought I'd come down and say hi."

"How did it go?" Matt asked.

"As well as can be expected, I think. It was good to see Chloe."

"Oh yes, I'd forgotten she was involved," Dilys said.

"They're a hard-working bunch but they do need, sort of, pulling together," Fabia said. "I'm not sure they've been working as a team, all too keen on protecting their own territory." Given the slight tension she could feel in Matt and his apparent lack of curiosity about her morning, she wished she hadn't said that. "I'm hoping to help them change."

She'd come around to stand beside Matt and glanced at the screen of his laptop, then stooped to get a better look. "I recognise that face," she said.

Matt gave her a sharp look. "Who is it?"

"That's Jake Seddon."

"You know him? In what context?" Matt asked.

"When was it?" Fabia said, frowning. "I'd say about seven years ago."

"Your memory always amazes me," Matt said, sounding a little resentful. "Dilys is the same."

"We're observant, us women," Fabia said. The look on Matt's face made her regret her comment immediately. She went on quickly, "I was working with Gwyn Jones. Do you remember him, Matt? He's retired now and attended that reunion dinner I went to a couple of weeks ago."

"Vaguely," Matt said. "He was pretty old school, wasn't he? Ex-army or something like that. That was about the time I was seconded to the Gloucestershire force, so I probably didn't come across him much."

"We had Seddon in on suspicion of possession with intent to supply," Fabia told him, "but we couldn't make it stick, and he walked. It really annoyed us at the time because we were sure he was up to his ears in the racket. But there it is, you win some, you lose some. Gwyn was really pissed off about it. He'd have liked to march him down to the cells and leave him there to rot. Gwyn moved on soon after, although I did see him at a funeral at St Cybi's a few months ago. Old Mr Pritchard's funeral, I think it was. Anyway, what's all this about?"

"Seddon is the one I told you about, the body that was found in the Usk railway tunnel on Tuesday," Matt told her. "We found out that there'd been a missing persons report, it came up from Bridgend, but we've only just made the connection."

"He was a nasty piece of work," Fabia said. "Do you think he got on the wrong side of another dealer?"

"Could be," said Dilys. "It's useful to have Fabia identify him, isn't it, sir?"

Fabia suppressed a smile. She could tell Dilys was trying to smooth things over, bless her. She decided that, given Matt's touchiness, it would be best to leave them to it, so said her goodbyes and headed out to the car park.

Matt turned to Dilys. "Can you get someone onto finding the information from that arrest? Fabia said seven years ago, it shouldn't be too hard to track it down."

"Will do, sir. I'll get Sara onto it."

A little later, Pat Curtis phoned Matt with her initial findings just as Inspector Kapoor came through about Jake Seddon. Matt spoke to the doctor while Dilys took the call from Kapoor.

"It's definitely a case of blunt force trauma," Pat Curtis told Matt. "Basically his skull was caved in. There's no residue in the wound from stone or wood, so he must have been hit with something smooth, probably metal."

"A hammer, perhaps?" Matt suggested.

"Possibly, that would certainly do the sort of damage we found. Furthermore, there were shallow cuts on his chest, made recently. It looks as if someone was trying to form letters, but I'm not entirely sure what. The first is a *C*, I think, and the second one could be a *M* or a *N*. They were inflicted before death and he was obviously restrained. There are dark bruises round his ankles and wrists, and in parts the skin has broken. As I told you, the middle fingers on his right hand had been broken." She took a deep breath. "Another thing, his lower leg bones have been smashed to pieces and there is significant damage higher up."

"Nasty," Matt said. "Sounds like someone took a baseball bat to him."

"I don't think so. The bones were broken after death as though he had been dropped – feet first – onto a hard surface."

"Okay, thank you, Doctor."

Matt stood frowning until Dilys finished her call to Inspector Kapoor.

"The inspector's going to send round a copy of Mrs Seddon's statement," she told him. "Obviously she was upset but apparently she said she wasn't surprised."

"How come?"

"She said he'd got some unpleasant friends and that he'd been threatened, something to do with the area he did his work, as she called it. When pressed, she admitted she didn't know exactly what work he did, but thought it was something to do with drugs since he was a pharmacist. She insisted it was legal."

"Then why the unpleasant friends?"

"Exactly, but she was adamant. The inspector said he thought she was holding information back."

"Something about the unlicensed drugs?"

"He didn't say, but he got the impression she wasn't that upset by her husband's death. Oh, and another thing. They conducted a comprehensive search of the house and found no mobile phone, laptop or any other device, other than Mrs Seddon's pretty basic mobile, which she insists she hardly ever uses."

"Did he say whether they found anything else, like bloodstains or whatever? You know Karen said she didn't believe he was killed in the tunnel."

"He didn't mention anything of the sort, but I'll double-check."

"Thanks, Dilys. Oh, and get a couple of uniforms back on site. I want to know how the killer moved the body there. Have them check for holes or vents in the roof of the tunnel."

"Rightio, sir."

Matt looked at the screen of his laptop, frowning, then looked up at Dilys who was waiting patiently in front of his desk.

"Have you remembered what was bugging you about the broken fingers?"

"No." She grimaced. "It's really annoying me. I'll let you know directly it comes back to me."

* * *

Cath was beginning to think that Fabia had been right about Huw Prosser. On Thursday morning, he'd pitched up on her doorstep with an enormous bunch of daffodils. The first moment she had, she phoned Fabia and told her what had happened.

"He said he'd come to wish me a happy St David's Day. I thought of you and how you told me once that you don't like flowers in a vase, you'd rather see them in a garden. So, I told him that was how I felt."

"Good idea, glad I could be of service," Fabia said.

"But it didn't work. He just said that was okay and asked me if I liked chocolates or fruit. He said he'd bring them next time. When I told him I'd rather he didn't bring me any gifts, he said he was sure I didn't mean that, and all this time he's standing far too close. He obviously wanted to be invited in."

"You didn't, did you?"

"No chance," Cath said. "He insisted he knew how 'you ladies' – ladies, mark you! – 'like gentlemen to bring gifts'. For goodness sake, he sounded like something from a P. G. Wodehouse novel. I told him he mustn't bring me anything more, that it wasn't appropriate."

"And what was his reaction?"

"That was rather worrying. He gave me such a look."

"What kind of look?" Fabia asked, sounding really concerned now.

"For a second, he looked really angry, and he stepped towards me. It was all rather threatening, then he gave me this broad smile and said, 'As you wish, but I won't give up. I shall remain hopeful.'"

"Did you tell him to piss off?" Fabia said hopefully.

"No, I just said I was sorry, but I had to get to work and closed the door on him."

"It's getting a bit out of hand, Cath. If you can't persuade him to back off, you're going to have to speak to the rural dean, see if he can get anywhere with the stupid man."

"I know."

"Talking of stupid men, I had my first meeting with the safeguarding team this morning."

"Full of stupid men?" Cath asked.

Fabia laughed. "No, only one. A probation officer called George Morris. I think he's one of those men who find women in authority threatening. I had a few run-ins with him way back, when I was an inspector. As far as I was concerned, a partnership between the police and the probation service could do nothing but good. I always felt he was pulling in the opposite direction, trying to protect his clients against me... us. We'll have to wait and see how it goes, but I definitely didn't get the impression he'd changed his ways."

"Bloody committees," Cath said with feeling. "There's always one, isn't there. What about the rest of them?"

"They were fine, as far as I could tell. Chloe Daniels is one of the team, which is helpful."

"That's good. I remember her when she was looking after Caleb Morgan's family, particularly at his funeral,"

Cath said, referring to a case Fabia and Matt had been involved in a year or two ago. "I was really impressed."

"Yes, she's a gem. And the others were a little wary but fine, so far."

"Just take it slowly," Cath said, then added, "but that's a case of teaching my grandmother to suck eggs. You'll be fine, and a great asset to the team."

"I do hope so," Fabia said.

"Come on, Fabia. You sound uncertain and that's not like you."

"Do I? Ah well, maybe it's new-mother insecurities."

Cath gave a derisive snort. "Don't give me that. You've been urging me to be assertive, you should take your own advice."

"Will do. Are you going to phone the dean then?"

"Yes, I will," Cath said decisively.

"Good, let me know what he says."

Fabia cut off the call and stood gazing out of the kitchen window, deep in thought. She loved the view from her kitchen. To the right were allotments where only a couple of hardy growers were to be seen on this cold March day. Through the tangled, leafless branches of an old apple tree, the fields stretched away from the bottom of her garden in a gradual upward slope. They were interrupted here and there by sheep, cream and occasionally black bundles of wool moving lazily about, cropping at the grass. In the distance, the fields gave way to a more sombre landscape as the lower slopes of the Black Mountains began to rise, and here the colours changed to misty blue, grey and mauve. Farther up, the distinctive shape of Sugar Loaf mountain was visible.

As she stood there, she wondered if she'd been right. Was she less sure of herself since Bethan had been born? Or was it the events of the last four years that had eaten away at her confidence? Surely, her renewed relationship with Matt and the clearing of her name should have given her back her self-esteem, let alone the birth of their child. She gave herself a little shake. Enough of this introspection. It wouldn't get her anywhere and worrying away at Cath's problem wouldn't help much either. She must get down to do some work. Her agent had been pestering her to complete the pen and ink illustrations she'd been commissioned to draw. She'd better get on with it.

From upstairs, she could hear Bethan's demands for attention after her nap. She thought she'd go upstairs and fetch her daughter, and let her play on the floor while she got on with her work, if Bethan allowed, of course. However, as she went up the stairs the negative thoughts still niggled away at her, so once she had settled her daughter, she went to the living room and picked up the phone.

"Hallo, Geraldine," Fabia said when her call was answered. "I hope I'm not disturbing you."

"Not at all, Fabia, always good to hear from you. Are you all well?"

"We are, thank you, although Bethan is teething so Matt and I could do with a little more sleep. How are things with you?" She hesitated then asked, "How is Frank?"

Frank, Geraldine's husband, was in a secure mental institution, having been found guilty of a murder. Fabia heard her friend take a deep breath.

"Much the same, but thanks for asking. No one ever does."

"I'm sorry, I should have been in touch before now, I know."

"Don't be silly, Fabia, you have a baby to care for – and a new job, I hear. Chairman of the LSCB. How is that going?"

"Early days yet but I am looking forward to getting stuck in."

"I'm sure."

"One of the reasons I'm ringing is I wanted to ask you about one of the parishioners at St Cybi."

"From a professional or personal point of view?"

"Bit of both, really, if I'm honest. As you know, Cath Temple and I are close friends and she's been struggling a little." Fabia chuckled in an attempt to lighten the mood. "It seems one of her sidesmen is paying her too much attention and I'm worried about her."

"Ah," Geraldine said. "I guess you might be talking about Huw Prosser. A couple of us have noticed. He can be a nuisance." She laughed. "One of my friends calls him Prosser the Tosser."

"What can you tell me about him?" Fabia asked.

"Not much, really, I reckon he's lonely. He joined the church maybe a couple of years ago now and from the start was happy to become involved."

"Do you know where he moved from?"

"No, I don't. He paid the single women more attention than he probably should, myself included, but once we made it plain we weren't interested, he gave up."

"I wish he'd leave Cath alone. She told me he rings her nearly every day and often brings flowers. She's not very happy with the situation, but feels she can't tell him where to go as she has responsibilities towards her parishioners."

"Men like him can be a pain, but I'm sure he's not dangerous. Cath just needs to be firmer and I'm sure he'll get the message. If you like, I'll keep an eye on him when I attend the services, provide Cath with some moral support."

"Would you? Oh that would be kind, thank you."

"No problem. We're a close-knit bunch at St Cybi's and take care of each other, you don't need to be worried. Now, tell me about little Bethan, I'd so like to meet her. Perhaps you could come over for lunch one day?"

"I'd like that, we'll have to book a date."

## Chapter 6

It wasn't until the following morning that Matt felt they were making some progress. The day before, he'd sent Inspector Kapoor the information DC Sara Gupta had downloaded about Seddon's investigation eight years ago. Kapoor had responded by sending them a copy of Mrs Seddon's statement, and a transcript of an interview with her when she'd been questioned at the time. Kapoor had also confirmed that there had been no evidence at all of bloodstains or any altercation when they searched the Seddons' house, nor had there been any evidence that drugs were manufactured on the premises.

It was now seven o'clock on Friday morning and he and Dilys had come into the office early so that they could go through the information they'd gathered so far. Silence reigned in the room, although they could hear the rest of the team arriving in the main office, talking as they got down to work.

After half an hour, Dilys sat back from studying the screen of her laptop and removed her earphones. She looked across at Matt.

"I've been listening to the recording of Fabia and Gwyn Jones's interrogation of Seddon. She certainly had an awesome interviewing technique," she said. "I love the way she used that quiet voice that makes people feel she's entirely on their side then, wham, picks their story to shreds."

Matt smiled. "I remember it well. I learnt a lot from her. It's a pity it doesn't seem to have worked on this Seddon bloke."

"Not enough to charge him," Dilys said, "but there's some useful information here. For instance, the connection to the Michaelson gang. It seems Dai and Paul Michaelson are his wife's cousins."

Matt looked across at her, eyebrows raised. "That's well worth checking up on. Where are they at the moment? Still banged up?"

"I'll check." Dilys pulled her laptop towards her, then stopped, her eyes widening. She slapped a hand to her forehead. "That's it!"

"What is?"

"The broken fingers. I remember now. Dai Michaelson ran a protection racket and that was one of his trademarks when somebody didn't pay up. I remember the last case that put him inside, GBH it was. It must have been, what, four or five years ago. Give me a moment, I'll bring up the details."

She tapped away at her laptop then turned it so that Matt could see the screen. On it was a report of a case of grievous bodily harm. The owner of a corner shop in Ringland was badly beaten, lucky not to have been killed. The shop was trashed and his fingers broken, but he'd refused to tell the police who was responsible. His wife, however, hadn't been so easily cowed. She'd managed to video some of the attack on her mobile and handed the evidence over to the police. Dai Michaelson had been arrested and ultimately sent down for eight years.

"He would have been released on licence earlier in the year after completing half his sentence, but he lost remission."

"Do you know why?" Matt asked.

"Attacked another inmate, battered him around the head and broke fingers on both of his hands. Seems old habits die hard. As far as I'm aware, his brother Paul hasn't been inside since 2016." Dilys closed her laptop. "I'll go and check, sir."

Within fifteen minutes, Dilys was back. "I was right, Paul Michaelson has been out since 2016, sir. He's managed to keep his nose clean, but I was right, his brother's still in prison. He's got another year at least before he can be considered for parole. Maybe Paul's decided to adopt some of his brother's habits."

Matt sat looking down at his desk, frowning and deep in thought. Then he looked up. "Right, Dilys. We'll have a word with both brothers. We'll also have a word with Mrs Seddon about her delightful cousins. Can you sort that out?"

"Will do, sir."

"And as soon as possible, please," Matt said. "Meanwhile I'm going to pick Fabia's brains about the Michaelsons. She may well remember something useful."

"Good idea," Dilys said, smiling her approval as she left his office.

Fabia picked up within a couple of rings when Matt phoned her. "A nasty pair, though Dai was by far the worst," she said when he mentioned the Michaelsons, "and it wasn't just them on that racket. Why do you ask about them?"

"Apparently Jake Seddon's wife is a cousin of theirs."

"Is she now? I suppose this Seddon chap could have got on the wrong side of them. I seem to remember that breaking people's fingers was one of Dai Michaelson's little habits."

"Yes," Matt said. "Dilys said the same."

"Which points in his direction for the Seddon murder so–"

"The trouble is," Matt interrupted her, "Dai's banged up, which is quite a good alibi."

"Ah. What about his brother? He was much more of a follower than a leader, although I always had the impression he wanted to be as tough as his brother. Dai was definitely the one in charge, but Paul might have come out of his shell while his brother has been in prison."

"It's possible. Can you think of anything else about him – or them?"

There was silence on the line, but Matt just waited, knowing that Fabia would answer his question once she'd thought it through.

After a few moments, she said, "I remember interviewing Dai once about an assault. He was slippery as an eel and I just couldn't dent his confidence. The only time I got under his skin was when I suggested he was leading his brother by the nose, forcing him to join in his criminality. That seemed to touch a nerve. I was very glad I wasn't alone with him. He got himself under control, but it was a glimpse of what he was capable of. That's probably why I remember it so clearly. Try playing one off against the other, that might get results."

"If I get the opportunity, I'll certainly do that."

"And it wasn't just the two brothers, their mother was a tough old bird," Fabia added. "It was quite an organisation they had going, mostly based in Ringland. All the information will be on record, won't it?"

"Yes, I just wanted your impressions."

"Any time, Matt," Fabia said, sounding pleased.

"And if you can think of anything else that might be useful, let me know."

"I'll make a few notes while Bethan's having her nap."

"Thanks, love."

Matt got up and shrugged on his coat as the phone rang. "Lambert," he said.

"It's Craig, sir, PC Evans. I've been out to the railway tunnel with DC Watkins and we've found something.

There is a hole in the roof a couple of meters from where the body was found. An old steam vent has been cut open and the undergrowth around it has been disturbed. I reckon you were right and the body was posted through. All the killer had to do then was go into the tunnel and drag the victim into the recess."

"Well done, constable. I'm heading out now, but I'll give SOCO a ring first. Wait there until Karen Johns arrives and show her what you've found."

"Yes, sir. Thank you, sir."

Matt put the phone down and went to find Dilys.

# Chapter 7

Having gone through the usual protocols – which Matt thought was an irritatingly slow process – and made contact with Gwyneth Seddon, Matt and Dilys made their way through Newport and on to the M4. The drive took them rather longer than they'd hoped due to the heavy Friday traffic. It was nearly two o'clock when they came off at junction 35 to Pencoed. Following the sat nav's instructions, they arrived at the address they'd been given in a quiet but rather downtrodden street of identical houses.

"Probably used to be council housing before Maggie Thatcher poked her nose in," Dilys said. Being a true daughter of the Rhondda valleys, the former prime minister was not one of her favourite people.

Dilys parked outside a semi-detached house, almost certainly built in the 1960s. The patch of front garden was neat but rather bare, no daffodils pushing their green shoots through and no evidence of any shrubs. The windows were shrouded with rather dingy lace curtains, and the front door was in need of a coat of paint.

Dilys rang the bell and they could hear an elaborate tune chiming inside. After a moment, they heard footsteps and the door opened. The woman who stood there was mousy in more ways than one. Her pointed nose and small, dark eyes, brown hair, and beige jumper and skirt, all added to the impression. The dark shadows under her eyes and the hand that gripped the door jamb showed the strain she was under.

"Mrs Gwyneth Seddon?" Matt enquired.

She nodded. "Yes?"

"I'm Chief Inspector Lambert, this is Sergeant Bevan," Matt told her. Both he and Dilys showed her their warrant cards. "I understand Inspector Kapoor informed you that we would be calling. Could we come in and have a word?"

Once again, she nodded. "Yes, I suppose so," she said and opened the door wider.

They followed her into a drab sitting room, devoid of pictures or family photos. A dark green three-piece suite was arranged symmetrically in front of an old-fashioned electric bar heater. Only the carpet stood out, its pattern a garish swirl of red and black.

Gwyneth sat down in one of the armchairs and waved a hand at the settee, indicating that Matt and Dilys should take a seat. "Why did you ask to speak to me? Inspector Kapoor told me you're based in Newport, not round here."

"That's right, but your husband's body was found in Usk," Matt said gently. "That means we are in charge of the investigation. We're very sorry for your loss, Mrs Seddon, and we will do our very best to find the person responsible."

"Thank you," she said, her voice so low they barely heard her.

"There are several points we would like to talk through with you," Matt continued, "but first would you mind if we record this interview? It's important we do so for our records."

"If you must," she said.

Dilys took out her iPad and placed it on the table, tapped away at it, giving the usual information, then nodded at Matt.

"First of all, have you any idea who might have done this to your husband?" he asked.

"No! Why would I?"

Matt thought this response a little strange. "Do you know if your husband had any enemies?" he went on. "Someone who may have wished him harm?"

Gwyneth didn't answer immediately, just sat looking down at her hands as she picked at a nail. Matt waited, hoping that not filling the silence would cause her to respond in the end.

"I suppose there could have been someone," she muttered, "but I don't know who."

"He might have mentioned being threatened," Matt said patiently, "or perhaps he told you about someone he was afraid of. You mentioned to Inspector Kapoor that he had some unpleasant friends."

"Did I? Well, I suppose I meant a couple of men that came to the house a few times." She sounded as if she was making it up as she went along. "I didn't like them, but I have no idea who they were. Jake always ordered me to go upstairs and stay there when they were around."

"And you did so?" Dilys asked.

"Yes. It was always best to do as Jake told me."

"Did you get the impression that he was afraid of these men?" Matt asked.

"I suppose he could have been, but Jake used to keep things to himself. He didn't talk about his work or that sort of stuff, or his… his friends.

"What was his work?" Matt asked.

"He trained as a pharmacist, but he didn't work at a chemist's. I think he worked for a pharmaceuticals company."

Dilys glanced at Matt but didn't need to say anything. Just that glance had reminded him of what the missing persons report had said. This information fitted with that. Was Gwyneth Seddon unaware that her husband had been suspected of manufacturing drugs illegally and selling them on? There was no way of knowing until they dug deeper. Given that Kapoor's officers had found no evidence, they'd have to look further afield for the location of Seddon's laboratory.

"Do you know what the company was called?"

"No, I don't. My husband was a very private man, Chief Inspector, and so long as he brought in the money each month, I didn't really care."

"Have you no idea at all?"

"Isn't that what I just said?" She sounded more animated now.

Dilys sat forward and asked quietly, "Would you say you and your husband had a good relationship?"

"Why do you ask me that?" She wouldn't look Dilys in the eye, just continued looking down and picking at her thumbnail.

Dilys sat patiently. In the end, Gwyneth said, "I suppose he did like to get his own way."

Matt changed tack. "Inspector Kapoor asked you about your husband being investigated some years ago on a charge of manufacturing drugs and selling them on the black market."

"That was when we lived in Newport."

"Can you tell us about that?"

"It was all a load of nonsense," she said, her voice sullen. "They had to let him go; they had no evidence."

"Have you any idea why they should think he'd been doing so?" Matt asked.

"No, and I don't want to know either."

"Do you think it had anything to do with your cousins, Dai and Paul Michaelson?" he added.

This certainly got her attention. She looked up and Matt saw that she had become even paler than she was before. There was fear in her eyes. "No, no, of course not," she insisted, her hands gripped tighter in her lap.

"We think that there's a possibility one of the brothers may have had something to do with your husband's death," he said.

"Oh no," she said, but she didn't sound as if she was denying the possibility, rather that this was something she didn't want to hear. "Why would you think that? Anyway" – now there was a tinge of triumph in her voice – "Dai is in prison and Paul is… is overseas."

"Where?" asked Matt, his voice sharper now.

"I don't know. I just know he's not at home, see, not in Wales."

"And who told you this?" Dilys asked.

Gwyneth's eyes looked quickly from Dilys to Matt and back again. She opened her mouth, then closed it again. A moment later she said, "Cari, their mother; she told me."

"And you're sure you don't know where Paul is?" Dilys persisted.

"Didn't I just say so?"

"We were given to understand," Dilys said, "that he was back living with his mother, your aunt, Cari."

"Well if he is, nobody told me," Gwyneth said quickly, and it was difficult to know if she was being truthful.

"Would you be kind enough to give us your aunt's address?" Matt asked.

"Why do you want it?"

"We would like to have a word with her."

"But I don't… she might not want–"

"We can find the address easily enough," Matt said, "but it would be helpful of you could let us have it. It would save us time."

There was a quiet stand-off for a few moments, then Gwyneth said, "Oh, alright, if you must. She lives in Newport, in the Conway Court flats on Elizabeth Street, number five."

Matt jotted it down. "Just one more question. Do you have your husband's laptop or a mobile phone he used?"

"I haven't come across either."

Matt nodded and got to his feet. "Thank you for your time, Mrs Seddon. We do regret having to put you through this questioning, but I'm sure you want us to find your husband's killer."

She didn't comment.

Dilys reached out for her iPad and, as she did so, asked, "Has Inspector Kapoor appointed a family liaison officer to help you?"

"He asked me if I wanted someone, but I refused. I'd rather just be left alone."

"We do sympathise," Matt assured her, "but I'm afraid the investigation has to take its course. If there is anything we can do to help, please make contact with us or Inspector Kapoor. Here's my card."

Gwyneth took it from him without comment, led them into the hall, then closed the front door on their heels with a snap.

As Dilys manoeuvred out of their parking spot, Matt said, "We must have a word with Paul and his mother sooner rather than later."

"Good idea, and perhaps–"

Matt's mobile interrupted them and Dilys listened to his side of the conversation.

"What? … Hold on, Tom. Dilys should hear this too, I'll put you on speakerphone."

"We've got another one, sir," Tom Watkins said.

"Another what?" Matt said, but he had a feeling he knew what Tom meant.

"Dead body," Tom told him. "A call just came in from someone who says he's a surveyor for the company that's bought that piece of wasteland up behind St Madoc's School in Pontygwyn. He found a body lying under some brambles. Two officers from uniform responded."

"So, who else has attended?"

"Glyn Evans, sorry, Inspector Evans, followed them up there after they called in. No identification of the victim has come in yet, and there was nothing on the body to give them a clue as to who it is. A white male, probably in his early thirties, is all we've got."

"Okay, we'll be back in about forty minutes, you can give me the rest then."

Matt cut off the call and glanced at Dilys. "Here we go again. Step on it, Dilys. We'll blue light it. The sooner we get back, the better."

Although their car was unmarked, it had three blue lights built in, one either side of the headlights, and one above the windscreen behind the rear-view mirror. Dilys activated them and put her foot down.

# Chapter 8

"Did Inspector Evans tell you if he could work out how the man died?" Matt asked Tom when they got back to the station. He, Tom and Dilys had gathered in Matt's office.

"Yes, sir, he says it's the same MO – head bashed in like the body in the tunnel," Tom said. "The SOCOs are up there now and they told him it looks as if he was tortured before being killed."

Matt raised his eyebrows. "In what way?"

"Severe bruising around his ankles and wrists, as if he'd struggled against being tied up," Tom said. "There were also shallow cuts on his chest and a couple of broken fingers, both of which link up with the tunnel man, don't they? If the cuts were meant to be legible, it hasn't worked. Unfortunately, if it is writing, it is indistinguishable, so there's not much to go on there, but it does look like it could be the same murderer."

"Could be," Matt said.

"Oh, and there's another thing, a distinctive tattoo on the back of his right hand, a spiderweb extending round the fingers with an eye in the middle of the web. Inspector Evans said it looked as if it was done quite recently. No ID found on the body. He's currently a John Doe."

"We need to get a photo of that and we'll conduct a door-to-door round the tattoo parlours, just in case it was done locally. We'd better extend that to South Wales as well. We might get an identification. Can you set that up, Dilys?"

"Will do."

"We'll have to wait for the post-mortem to get more info," Matt said, thinking aloud. "There's definitely some kind of pattern here, but there's no way of making a firm connection, if there is any, until we know who this second victim is."

Matt clicked away at his laptop and brought up the photo that had been circulated when Jake Seddon went missing.

"Can you get me a photo of the body on the wasteland, Tom?" Matt grimaced. "Of as much of his face as remains, that is. Who's in charge of the SOCO team?"

"Karen Johns, same as before."

"Good. Give her a ring and ask her to send one asap. I want to find out if Jake Seddon and this man look alike – other than the injuries, that is. Also, ask her what she found – if anything – when she took another look at the first scene."

When the photo came through, Matt put them side by side on the screen of his laptop. He, Tom and Dilys stood studying the photos, the first one of a man with a boxer's nose and the strange pigmentation on one side of his face. The second photo was harder to judge, given that one side of the face was so damaged, but the skin was very pale. This, of course, could be as a result of the attack. The hair on the undamaged side was long and wispy, and the cheek thin and a little sunken. There was no similarity between the two men, none at all, except for the damage that had been done to them. Some of which was the signature injury inflicted on his victims by Dai Michaelson. But Dai was in prison. His brother, however, was not.

* * *

"I think a word with Paul Michaelson and his mam is long overdue," Matt said to Dilys later that afternoon.

"I agree," Dilys said. "Have we got the personnel?"

"You're a mind-reader. I was just thinking it'd be best to take backup, given who we're dealing with. We'll go in my car, Tom and Craig can follow in a squad car. It's a quarter to five now so, by the time we get there, chances are they'll be at home. Right. Let's get going. On the way, I'll give Fabia a ring and tell her I'm going to be late yet again."

Dilys gave him a sympathetic look but didn't comment.

It took them a while to get through the Friday rush-hour traffic, so it was close to six o'clock when they drew up in front of the three-storey block of flats. The whole building looked as if it was in sore need of repair. An effort had been made to cheer up the rectangular block with brightly painted front doors, but this just accentuated the building's dilapidation. Between the road and the flats was a scrubby patch of grass that definitely needed re-seeding. On each floor, a balcony stretched the length of the building, and even the ground floor had a railed-in walkway. Outside, washing was draped over clothes dryers. The whole place had a depressing air about it.

Having parked up, the four of them made their way along the walkway until they got to a yellow front door. Matt rang the bell. A curtain twitched in a window beside the door and they had just enough time to see a thin-featured man glance out, then quickly disappear. The door stayed firmly shut.

As Matt rang the bell again, he said to Tom and Craig, "Stand ready in case he tries to leg it." Then he knocked hard on the door and called, "Police. Open up."

Several neighbours looked out of their windows. The next-door neighbour opened her door and said, "They're at home. I saw them go in just now."

"Them?" Dilys asked.

"Cari and her boy, Paul."

Dilys glanced at Matt. "Not abroad then, sir."

At that moment the yellow door opened.

"Alright, alright!" A bulky woman with a thick neck and short, dark hair stood in the doorway, hands on her hips, her small eyes defiant. "What do you want?" she demanded.

"Mrs Cari Michaelson?" Matt asked.

"Yes. What do you want?" she repeated.

"Could we come in and have a word with you and your son?"

"You can have a word with me, if you must, but my boy's down at his girlfriend's."

"I don't think so," Matt said. "We just saw him through the window."

"What do you mean? I tell you he's not here."

Dilys spoke quietly to the woman. "Let's go inside. I'm sure you don't want to attract too much attention from your neighbours."

For a moment, Cari glared at them, then she stepped aside.

Matt and Dilys followed her into the flat and she took them to the living room. They noticed that two armchairs were pulled up to a low table. On the table were two plates with the remains of pizzas on each. A can of beer stood beside one, a can of coke by the other. An enormous television screen faced the chairs showing a football match continuing busily, but with no sound. Cari scooped up the plates and went through a door at the back of the room. When she returned, she picked up the Coke can, took a drink, then sat down in one of the chairs and stared resentfully up at Matt and Dilys.

"So, what do you want?" she demanded. "Grab two of those chairs by there, you're making the place look untidy."

They did as she suggested. Matt leant forward, resting his elbows on his knees, his hands clasped lightly.

"Mrs Michaelson, it's obvious that you and your son were eating when we arrived, so where is he?"

"He had to go out."

"We know he's still here, Mrs Michaelson." Matt summoned Tom and Craig. "In here, you two, and take a look around."

Cari glared at Matt. "What d'you want with my boy? Are you going to fit him up like you did my eldest?"

There was a sound of voices from the back of the flat. Cari jumped up, looking alarmed. Matt and Dilys also rose to their feet. A moment later, Tom and Craig appeared in the living room escorting a tall and rather scruffy-looking man. His head was shaved and his T-shirt and trousers could have done with a wash.

"Found him in one of the wardrobes, sir," Tom said.

Matt resisted the urge to say 'Mr Paul Michaelson I presume', opting instead for, "I am Chief Inspector Lambert, this is Sergeant Bevan and these two officers you've obviously already met. Tell me, Mr Michaelson, why did you hide when you saw us at the front door?"

Paul Michaelson kept his mouth shut.

"Answer my question please," Matt said calmly.

All Matt got was silence and a sullen stare.

"Okay," Matt said. "We'll continue this down at the station."

"You can't do that!" Cari shouted. "You have nothing on him."

"Your son will be helping us with a current enquiry," Matt said.

"I know what that means, I do," she said with heavy scorn. "You're all bullies, you lot, bullies. You've harassed my family for years."

While his mother complained bitterly, they escorted Paul out to the police car and Tom and Craig set off with their reluctant passenger. Matt and Dilys followed. When they arrived at the station, Matt suggested they leave Paul Michaelson to cool his heels for a bit.

Once they'd established that nothing further had come in yet about the body on the wasteland, and they'd just have to wait for Karen Johns' report, Matt and Dilys went down to the interrogation room. Tom, who'd been keeping an eye on Paul Michaelson, let them into the grey-painted, dreary room. Recording equipment sat at one end of a metal table that was flanked by four chairs, two on each side. A small window, over which a blind was pulled down, faced the door, and there was a clock on the wall.

Paul jumped up from one of the chairs. "What you keeping me here for? This is a false fucking arrest, this is. I know my rights. I'm going–"

"Sit down, Mr Michaelson," Matt said, quietly but firmly.

Paul threw himself back into the chair, muttering as he did so.

Matt and Dilys went around the table and sat down. Dilys calmly set up the recording equipment, and gave the date and who was present, as Paul sat there glaring at them.

"If you hadn't tried to evade us, we wouldn't have had to bring you in," Dilys told him.

"I was getting ready to go out."

"Halfway through your meal?" Matt said, eyebrows raised. "I don't think so."

"What's that got to do with it? I'd had enough."

"Mr Michaelson," Matt said patiently. "You obviously know that your brother is in prison and why he is there."

Yet again, his only response was a sullen stare.

"Am I right in thinking that Dai had a habit of breaking people's fingers if they didn't cough up protection money?"

"You should know. You've got the records. They was lying, but you lot believed them."

"The judge and jury in court believed them too," Matt pointed out. "We just handed him over for trial. An important distinction."

Paul's only reaction to this was to sneer at Matt. Dilys wasn't sure he'd understood what Matt said.

She leant forward and rested her arms on the table. "Paul – may I call you Paul?"

He didn't reply, just shrugged.

"We are investigating two murders," she told him, "and we're hoping you will be able to help us with our enquiries."

"Murders!" There was panic in his voice. "I got nothing to do with no murders."

"You may know one of the victims. Jake Seddon, your cousin Gwyneth's husband," Dilys said. "I'm sure she will have told you or your mother about his death."

"She did, kinda, but what's that got to do with me? I didn't even like him." Realising this might not reflect well on him, quickly he added, "But that doesn't mean I'd do him in, no way."

"Did you know that Jake Seddon had been questioned about manufacturing drugs illegally?" Dilys asked him.

"No." Paul crossed his arms across his chest almost as if he was protecting himself from their questioning.

Matt held up a photo of the tattoo on the second victim. "Do you know anyone with this tattoo?"

"No."

Matt was inclined to believe him as there wasn't a shadow of recognition in Paul's face.

"When did you last see your brother?" asked Matt.

"Couple of months ago. Me and mam went to visit him."

"Did you talk about the reason he's in prison? That he extorted money from several small businesses and then broke the fingers of people who wouldn't pay up?"

"I told you, he never," Paul said, slamming his fist down on the table in front of him. "They was lying bastards."

"Have you taken over where he left off?" Matt asked imperturbably. "Are you doing his dirty work while he's banged up?"

"So, you're going to frame me as well, are you?"

"No one is going to be or has been framed, Paul," Dilys said mildly. "Why don't you tell us why you really hid from us? If there's an innocent reason, then we can all go home."

He seemed to be more co-operative when Dilys was asking the questions. "I thought you was going to arrest me."

"And why would you think that?"

"Cos that's what you lot do, isn't it?"

"Not without reason," Dilys said. "Do you think there's a reason why we should do so, Paul?"

"'course not.

"What we are thinking, Paul," Matt said, "is that you might believe it's a good idea to do as your brother did. Prove what a tough bloke you are."

"Do what Dai– what d'you mean?"

It occurred to Matt that the youngest Michaelson wasn't the sharpest knife in the drawer. This interrogation was getting them nowhere. He leant forward in his chair and tried again.

"The two murders we're investigating, that of your cousin-in-law and another victim, have similarities," Matt told him patiently. "One of these is that both had their fingers broken, just as your brother did to his victims. Have you decided to follow in his footsteps?"

"I haven't– I don't– what are you suggesting?" He still didn't seem to have made the connection between what Matt had told him and his questions. But a second later, it dawned on him, and he jumped up. Tom stepped forward, ready to intervene.

"You're making it all up. You can't accuse me, you bastard!" Paul shouted.

"Sit down," Matt said. "Sit down, now."

Paul slumped back into his chair, glaring at Matt.

"So you're telling us you had nothing to do with these deaths?" Dilys asked quietly.

"'course I am. What do you take me for?"

Matt looked at Dilys then nodded towards the door. Dilys excused them both from the interview and followed Matt out into the corridor, closing the door behind them.

"This is a waste of time, Dilys."

"That's what I was thinking. Not the brightest in the bunch, is he?"

"He may be responsible, but we need motive – which we haven't got – and forensics to put him at the scenes of both crimes."

"We should have his DNA on file," Dilys pointed out. "It wasn't long ago that he was arrested and fined for driving under the influence, and he's been in prison."

"True, his fingerprints will be on file too. Okay. We'll hand that information over to Karen and ask her to double-check, but for now I don't think we can hold onto him."

"Do you want to let him go then?" Dilys asked.

"I think that's what we're going to have to do. Can you tell Tom? I'll go and e-mail Karen."

Dilys turned back to the interrogation room while Matt made his way back upstairs to his office.

# Chapter 9

By Monday they still hadn't managed to identify the second body. Karen and Pat Curtis both thought that he had been dead somewhat longer than Jake Seddon had when he was found, but an exact time of death was difficult to establish. The weather had been colder, so decomposition would have been slower. Nor had they had any luck with the search through the tattoo parlours. On that, they would just have to keep going.

Matt decided to arrange a press conference to appeal for information, and provide a detailed description of the man. That happened first thing and, halfway through the afternoon, Dilys took a call from the owner of a Chinese takeaway in Usk. He told her that he had a tenant renting a room above the garage behind his restaurant who fitted the description they had given. He said that his tenant hadn't paid his rent for the current month, it had become due nearly a week ago. In the past, he'd always paid on time, sometimes a day or two early. Mr Cheng had texted him several times but had received no reply. In the end, he'd gone up to knock on his door, but there had been no answer.

"When I tried the door handle, I found the room was unlocked, but when I went in there was no sign of Mr Geddings."

"Did you say his name was Geddings, sir?" Dilys asked.

"Yes, Seth Geddings. That description you gave on the news this morning, it was very similar to him. Thin body; long, fair hair, which he usually tied back; in his early thirties. Just the same."

"Thank you very much for contacting us, Mr Cheng," Dilys said. "Please, don't move anything in the room, and would you lock the door, please? We'll send someone round to have a look."

"I will do as you ask. I will be here for the rest of the day."

Dilys's eyes widened, and she went straight to Matt's office. "We've just had a call from a Mr Chen. He recognises the man you described in the press conference as a Seth Geddings. The name was in that NFIB report that came in last week; there was a photo with it."

Matt turned to his computer and tapped away for a minute or two. "Bingo!" he said. "Stupid. I should have checked this before. Does this remind you of anyone?"

She came around the desk to look and nodded slowly. "It could be. There's the same straw-coloured hair, thin features. We'll have to show this to Mr Cheng, see if he recognises him."

Dilys decided to go to Usk herself and take PC Craig Evans with her; it would be good experience for him. They were lucky enough to find a parking spot just outside the Lotus Flower restaurant and takeaway, and a diminutive, smiling Chinese man ushered them in. His accent was an interesting mixture of his native Cantonese and Welsh. Dilys recognised him as the man who'd made the call.

"Could we have a word before we go to see the room?" Dilys asked.

"Of course, please come to my office." He led them through the kitchen where two young men and an older woman were busy stirring large saucepans and industriously chopping vegetables. They gave the police officers curious looks as they passed but did not comment. There was an all-pervading smell of Chinese food throughout the building.

"Makes me hungry," Craig murmured to Dilys.

Mr Cheng led them to a tiny office at the back which, if it hadn't been scrupulously tidy, would not have been big enough for all three of them. He waved them to plastic chairs and went to sit behind a small desk. On the wall behind it was a colourful poster advertising Hong Kong as a holiday destination. Beside it hung a photograph of Queen Elizabeth in full regalia.

"Do you mind if I record our conversation on my iPad?" Dilys asked him.

"Not at all, please to do so. I know my civic duty."

I wish everyone did, Dilys thought.

She placed the iPad on the desk, stated the date and who was present, then swiped the screen and turned the tablet around so that Mr Cheng could see a photo of Seth Geddings. "Is this your tenant?"

Mr Cheng leant forward and peered at the screen. "He looks quite different to the last time I saw him, but yes, I think that's Mr Geddings."

"How long has he been living here?" Dilys asked.

"About a year. I could ask my wife to check the exact date in the rent book. She keeps a very good record of rent paid and any other expenses incurred by his tenancy."

He jumped up, opened the door and called out in a stream of Cantonese and an answer came from the kitchen. He returned to his chair and sat down just as the woman they had seen chopping vegetables came into the room. She placed a small blue book in front of her husband, gave them a shy smile, then left.

"My wife, she does not like computers. I keep telling her she should keep her records on the computer, but she says no." He gave a shrug and reached for the notebook. "Ah yes, his last payment was at end of January."

"Do you know what work he does?" Dilys asked.

"I think it is something to do with computers, but I don't know exactly. We have not seen him go out very often, but as the stairs to his room are on the other side of the garage, we may not notice him going out and coming in. He has a very expensive computer in his room, two screens, all very up to date. My son tells me it costs a lot of money, which is why I thought maybe he works from home. Many people do nowadays."

"Very true," Dilys said. "Does he have any family that you know of?"

"I believe he does. He told me he came from Tredegar but that he had a– what did he call it? A falling out with his family and that was when he moved to Usk. I do not know if his parents are still alive."

Craig sat forward, glanced at Dilys for permission, then asked, "Did he tell you what happened with his family?"

"Not really. He was a very quiet young man, but always polite to me and my wife."

"I think we had better have a look at his room now, Mr Cheng," Dilys said. "Would you show us where it is?"

"Yes, please follow me."

Mr Cheng manoeuvred through the small gap between his desk and the wall and went to the door. Dilys picked up her iPad and she and Craig followed him to where the back door was open at the end of the rather gloomy hallway. They went out, passing a neat row of dustbins and stacked cooking-oil cans in the backyard. There was what looked like a garage, but Mr Cheng did not open it. Instead, he went around to the other side of the building and led them up a flight of metal stairs. He opened a door at the top. Inside there was a small hallway and two doors leading off it. He unlocked one of them and pushed it open.

"I'm afraid Mr Geddings was not a tidy man," he said.

"No worries," Dilys said, then added, "thank you, sir. We won't keep you from your work."

Mr Cheng hesitated, then gave them a little bow and went back down the stairs, glancing back at them as he did so.

Dilys and Craig stood in the doorway.

"Not exactly homely, is it?" Craig said.

Dilys grimaced. "You could say that."

They both pulled on gloves and put protective covers on their shoes then stepped into the room. Craig flicked on the light switch by the door and a single bulb hanging from the ceiling lit up. The floor was covered with a clean but shabby grey carpet and the bed to one side was unmade, all the covers pulled back to reveal the mattress beneath. There were a couple of chairs – one lying on the floor on its side – and an armchair covered in a throw. A microwave oven stood on a cupboard in the corner. In contrast to the shabbiness and the cheap furniture, an expensive-looking office chair stood before the desk. The things that stood out most were the two gleaming computer screens, a keyboard, a computer, and an expensive laptop – all on a desk in front of the only window.

"Look over there," Dilys said, pointing towards the desk and the fallen chair. "Can you see those dark spots on the carpet?"

"Yes. I see them."

"I think they might be blood."

Craig's eyes widened. "Could be."

Dilys put an arm out to stop Craig going further into the room. "I think we need to get Karen's SOCO team in here. It's best we don't start stomping around ourselves."

"Okay, Sarge," he said, sounding a little disappointed.

"We'll have to stay here and make sure no one goes into the room. Could you go and explain what's happening to Mr Cheng?"

"Will do," Craig said and made his way back down the stairs.

Dilys took out her phone and tapped in Matt's number. She was relieved when he picked up after a couple of rings.

* * *

When the SOCO team arrived at the back door of the restaurant, Dilys brought them up to date. Having arranged for Craig and another uniformed officer to stand guard outside, she returned to the station. Karen's team spent several hours searching the room, the staircase and the backyard, going over every centimetre and bagging up anything interesting. They also put all the computer equipment, any paperwork, some clothes and other personal effects into large plastic bags. At six o'clock that evening, Matt's phone rang as he was about to leave the office. It was Karen Johns.

"We've done the initial search, but there was a distinct lack of personal bits and bobs. No photos of family, very little paperwork apart from some computer magazines. A box of teabags, some instant coffee, sugar, but that's all. It's as if he was just camping out. And of course a bunch of top-end computer stuff."

"Strange. Mr Cheng said he's been their tenant for a year, you'd think there'd be odds and ends about the place."

"Exactly, but we haven't come away empty-handed. There's more to do," she told him, "but I thought you'd like an update. So far, we've found traces of blood, as your sergeant suggested, on the carpet about two feet from the desk, we may find more, but I don't think he was killed in that room. There were a couple of drops of blood on the floor and on the chair, and a couple more in the hallway and on the stairs, but no spatters in evidence as there would have been had he been hit, say, while sitting at his desk. I think the drops of blood could have come from the cuts on his chest. We've collected some hair samples as well. The DNA results will take a bit longer, as you know. Oh, and we found some sticky residue on the arms of his office chair, possibly from gaffer tape."

"It's looking increasingly like the body from the waste ground and Mr Cheng's tenant are one and the same, doesn't it? I'll get Aidan Rogers to work on the computer and laptop." Aidan was an IT expert who often worked on Matt's cases. "Did you find a mobile?"

"Yes. It was a bit strange. We found it taped to the back of a drawer in the desk. It was just a cheap burner phone like the ones that drug dealers use. We also found an envelope full of SIM cards in the drawer, but no iPhone or smartphone."

"Hopefully they will give us some information," Matt said. "Hand it all over to Aidan and he'll work his usual magic. Anything else?"

"That's all at the moment. My team is still combing the place, but I don't think we'll find much more. I'll get my report done as quickly as possible."

"Thank you, Karen."

Once he'd ended the call, Matt sat with his chin on his clasped hands, staring into space and going over what Karen had told him. At least now they had a chance of positively identifying the second body. The trouble was Geddings wasn't an unusual name in these parts, so finding the man's family wouldn't be easy.

At that moment, Dilys came into his office. "I've just had a call from Mr Cheng, sir. He says his wife told him their tenant once mentioned a sister. It was a couple of months ago when she'd been concerned about him being able to pay the rent and he told her not to worry. He said if he didn't have enough money himself, he could always ask his sister for a loan. She asked him where his sister lived, and he said Swansea. Unfortunately, that's all she knows. If she goes by a married name, it won't help us."

"Well, let's hope Aidan comes up with more from the victim's devices and the burner phone." Matt described what Karen had told him then frowned across at Dilys. "I wonder why he'd hidden it."

"Probably because there's potential evidence recorded on it."

"With any luck, it'll turn up a few fingerprints if nothing else."

## Chapter 10

Halfway through the following morning, Aidan walked into Matt's office. "Have you got a moment, sir?"

"Yes, have a seat," Matt said.

The flimsy office chair protested as Aidan lowered his considerable bulk into it. As he sat down, he muttered something about having to lose weight.

Matt didn't think it was appropriate to comment. Instead he asked, "Have you got anything useful for me?"

Aidan put his laptop on the desk. "I started with the burner phone," he said. "There's very little on it, but then it can't store much anyway. There's a list of contacts – obviously a code. There's Snow White, Robin, Batman and Minions Three, to name but a few. When I tried the numbers, I didn't get any response, so that device hasn't coughed up anything that useful. I've checked the number on the SIM with the provider and they confirmed it was switched on for the first time in Usk." He sighed heavily. "The point of a burner phone is anonymity. The device, SIM card and any credit were more than likely bought with cash, to be untraceable, probably at different locations. Of course, the buyer doesn't have a contract or have to provide identity to make the purchases."

"What about the computer and laptop, and the extra SIM cards?"

"I think they'll be more interesting. We're definitely dealing with a serious scammer here."

"He must have been a serious scammer. This is the man the NFIB was after."

Matt went to the door of his office. "Dilys, we need your input."

"Yes, sir." A moment later she had settled herself in a chair next to Aidan.

"Listen to what Aidan has to say," Matt suggested.

"It looks like this Seth Geddings character was hiding behind several authentic-sounding company names and promising big dividends to investors, but the companies don't exist. He'd even stolen the identity of a respected London solicitor using her Facebook page and website. Basically he was promising fantastic returns to his targets. He said he had access to his uncle's gold mine in South Africa, but needed finance up front to pay for equipment, licences, whatever, before he could rake in the loot and hand over their 'share'. I've found a spreadsheet in the documents from the NFIB which has provided us with the names of the companies and the amounts of money people have been 'investing'." Aidan mimed inverted commas in the air. "I hope to have it ready for you soon." He wiped a hand over his face. "Geddings didn't stop there either. He was also running romance scams."

"A busy boy," Dilys said, her voice a mixture of disgust and anger.

"Yes, he was," Aidan agreed. "I've found at least three poor saps–"

Matt gave Aidan a sharp look and interrupted him. "I'm not sure that terminology is appropriate, Aidan," he said, thinking of what Fabia had told him about Cath's activities on the dating site. "There are a lot of lonely people – male and female – out there, who can be taken in by these shits."

"Sorry, sir. You're right, of course. Anyway, he's been posing as a woman with one bloke." He turned the laptop around so that Matt and Dilys could see a photo on the screen of a voluptuous, dark-haired woman. The T-shirt she was wearing was definitely a little too small and revealed a very generous cleavage. "He calls himself Courtney. There are several WhatsApp conversations between him, as Courtney, and someone called Frank Williams – given that name, it could be a pseudonym."

"That's probably quite common," Dilys pointed out. "Even if a person thinks this is a legitimate relationship, some may not want to use their real name; possibly ashamed, deep down, to be in thrall to someone online that they've never met."

"Well, he's milked this poor bloke of a tidy sum of money, about £50,000, I'd say. What's more, there are two women he's got on a string as well, one of whom seems to be based in South Wales, given her phone number which she's put in one of their exchanges. In those exchanges he calls himself Clint and has a picture of a Clint Eastwood lookalike!"

"Oh, for goodness sake!" Dilys muttered.

Aidan gave her a lopsided smile. "Bit obvious, isn't it. Anyway, this poor woman was begging him to contact her. He hooked her with a sick-mother scam, can't afford treatment, NHS waiting lists are awful, so he has to go private because his mother will die if he doesn't get the money, etc. Communication with her stopped abruptly about a month ago."

"Lucky for her," Matt muttered.

"Could she have found out where he lived?" Dilys asked.

"I doubt it," Aidan said. "There's no evidence they met up or that he broke his cover in her case."

The phone rang and Dilys had a brief conversation, then hang up. "Mr Cheng's wife has just had her husband call. She's remembered the name of Geddings' sister," she said. "Apparently she lives in Sketty, Swansea, and her name is Lois Clarke. Geddings gave her name as a referee, but not her full address. She'll have to be informed, won't she? Shall I get on to Swansea Central?"

"Do that, Dilys, thank you," Matt said, "that's a couple of steps forward. We must pool all the information we have on these victims and see if there's any link between them. Meanwhile, can you put all this into a spreadsheet, Aidan?"

"I've started that, nearly finished."

"Good man. Send it through to me and I'll take it up to show the boss," Matt said. "We must get on to the NFIB, find out if they've sent us everything they've got and go from there."

"That won't help us with the connection between the two victims," Dilys said.

"True. If there is one."

"There must be, sir, what with the cutting on their chests and the broken fingers."

"I know, I know, but what? Why these individuals? The only other things that link them are the fact they have both broken the law and, so far, got away with it – and, of course, they lived in this area." Matt ran a hand through his hair, as he frowned across at her. "I just wish we had more to go on."

Matt's phone clamoured for attention and he glanced at the screen. "It's Fabia, I'd better answer it."

Dilys and Aidan made themselves scarce.

Matt answered the call. "Hallo, love. What's up? Is Bethan okay?"

Fabia laughed. "She's fine. You always think when I phone during the day that there's something wrong with her."

"I know. I'm a fussy father."

"You are," she said, and he could tell she was smiling. "No, it's not our little chick I'm phoning about. I've been thinking about the Seddon case – well, cases past and present – and I've been wondering if it might be worth me getting in contact with my ex-colleague Gwyn Jones, find out if he remembers anything that could be useful."

Matt frowned, wondering if he should involve Fabia, and why he was reluctant to do so; after all, she'd been deeply involved in some other cases of his in the last few years. Of course, he could be the one to make contact. There was sure to be a record of Gwyn's present whereabouts if only for pension purposes.

Before he had the chance to tell her what he thought, Fabia said, "Your silence indicates you don't think I should."

"How would you contact him?" Matt asked.

"I know he moved to a desk job in the Chepstow force for a bit, and I'm sure he told me at the reunion dinner he had moved to the Mumbles when he took early retirement. I've got a mobile number on my phone from way back. He may not have changed it. I could give him a ring."

"I'm not sure I should involve you," Matt said cautiously.

"You've done so before, Matt," Fabia said, sounding offended.

"I know, it's just that–"

"Just what?" Fabia snapped.

"I'll think about it," Matt said, avoiding the question.

"Well, there was something else. Do you want to hear about that or not?"

Matt winced at her tone of voice. This was going from bad to worse. "Of course I do. Any help gratefully received, ma'am."

The joke fell flat.

"That time Gwyn and I had Seddon in wasn't the only time I interviewed him," Fabia said, her tone cool. "There were a pair of twins, girls, who ended up dead after a night out in Newport. The PM revealed that they'd both been taking a particular drug, a bit like Ecstasy but much stronger, and they overdosed. We had Seddon in because we thought he was one of the most likely people to have created this poisonous stuff, but, as before, we had to let him go for lack of evidence. He was distinctly unhelpful when it came to pointing us in the direction of anyone else who may have been responsible."

"And was Gwyn Jones involved in that case?"

"No, it was after he'd retired," Fabia said. "I think it was one of the first cases that Lewis Powell and I worked on together."

"The Lewis Powell that's now a Chief Inspector with the Powys force?"

"That's him. It might be worth having a word with him."

"Do you remember the names of the two girls?"

"Not off the top of my head," said Fabia. "Get Dilys or Sara to do a bit of digging for you. I think it was in 2015, round about then anyway, not long before my enforced sick leave."

"Thanks. I'll get on to it."

Matt ended the call, feeling annoyed with himself for being tactless and with Fabia for not understanding his reservations. He pushed himself up from his chair and went into the main office.

"Dilys, can you do a search for two deaths from overdose? Around 2015, Fabia says it was. Twin girls." Matt explained what Fabia had told him.

Dilys grimaced. "I'll have a look. It makes me a good deal less sorry for him if he was the one who created the drugs."

"But we still need to find his killer," Matt said. "If this person is working to a pattern, it's not beyond the bounds of possibility that we'll have another victim sooner rather than later."

"Give me a minute, sir. I'll see what I can do."

# Chapter 11

Matt got home late, yet again. Fabia knew that she should be more understanding having been in his position. Been there, done that, got the T-shirt she told herself, but she still felt resentment niggling away at her, particularly after their conversation earlier that day. When she was doing the same job as Matt, there'd been no Bethan to contend with, but Bethan's arrival didn't seem to have affected his work. She did her best to suppress her irritation, and felt it diminish when he said, "I hate missing Bethan's bath and bedtime. Did she go down okay?"

Fabia sighed. "More or less," she told him.

"I'll just go and have a quick look at her."

"Don't wake her," Fabia warned as he headed up the stairs.

When he got back downstairs, she poured glasses of wine for them both. "Have you eaten?"

"Yes," Matt said. "I should have let you know."

"Yes, you should," Fabia said dryly.

"I'm sorry. Won't happen again," Matt said. "Dilys got sandwiches brought in for all of us."

Fabia realised how stressed he was. "Let me pour you a glass of wine," she said. "I don't know what you'd do without Dilys, you're bloody lucky to have her. Worth her weight in gold, she is." She handed him the drink.

"Thanks, you're not wrong," Matt said.

"So, have you made any progress?" Fabia asked.

"Some. Did I tell you about the spiderweb tattoo we found on the second victim's hand?"

"No, you didn't."

Matt described it to her, and Fabia shook her head. "An appropriate image for a scammer – reaching out in a threatening way and the eye in the middle describes his activities rather well."

"That's more or less what Dilys said," Matt said. "The two of you often think along the same lines. Anyway, we've finally found the tattoo parlour he went to, a place in Cardiff, and spoken to the person who did this one – a woman called Lynette. I'm told by Sara that they're called artists and I suppose that's appropriate, body art and all that."

"Did you get any useful information from this tattoo artist?"

"A bit. She identified Seth Geddings and said she'd done the tattoo over two sessions. The last one was just over four weeks ago. She said the design was Geddings' own and he'd been talking about it being appropriate to his work – so you and Dilys are probably right. He also told her he'd be leaving Usk soon. He said he'd come into some money and was planning to do some travelling."

"At least you've got two firm identifications now," Fabia said.

"Yes, and that's not all. Dilys was able to arrange a visit to Dai Michaelson and he had a lot to say for himself, although not much of it was of any use. He didn't recognise Geddings and swore he hadn't heard anything from Jake Seddon for years and didn't know anything about the drugs. Otherwise, he just had gossip concerning his brother, mainly. Apparently, Paul was working as a bouncer in a Bristol nightclub, but lost the job and that's why he went back to live with his mother in the flat. Paul had said the staff at the nightclub were a lily-livered bunch and objected to him being 'firm' with the clients, which sounds as if he overstepped the mark. I still think that Paul might well want to take over where his tougher, older brother left off, and keep the business running."

"It's possible," said Fabia. "But it wouldn't really fit with what I remember of Paul's character. Very much a follower."

"That's the impression Dilys and I got."

"I doubt that he had an original idea in his head," Fabia went on. "On the other hand, maybe one of the others in the gang were responsible for the murders. I've made some notes, as promised. Do you want to have a look at them, or would that be interfering?"

"Fabia!"

"Sorry," she said with a sheepish grin.

"You know I value your input, it's just that–"

"Okay, forget it," Fabia said and passed a wirebound notebook across to him. "There's not much. I think you know most of it already. I've included some points about Jake Seddon too. And I've listed the names of a few of the Michaelsons' pals, those that I remember, that is."

Matt leafed through the pages covered in Fabia's distinctive handwriting. When he'd done so, he went back to one particular point on the second page.

"This bit about Jake Seddon manufacturing drugs for others to distribute. I know it's all circumstantial evidence, but it might be worth having a word with some of the known dealers. Have a sort of check-up on some that we've pulled in before. If they think they're going to be held responsible for his activities, they might cough up some useful information. Or they might think we believe one of them is the killer. You never know, although it's a while since his arrest, and the turnover rate of street dealers is pretty high."

"It's worth a try," Fabia said. "When it comes to the other bloke, Seth Geddings, did you get any more out of the NFIB?"

"Yes, that was useful. I spoke to one of their senior investigators. They've been monitoring this scammer for quite a while. They initially got wind of him because someone was brave enough to admit they'd been a victim and gave them a name. Not Seth Geddings, some rather unlikely pseudonym, but when they dug further, they found that the bank account this money was going into was in Newport under the name of S W Geddings." Matt ran a hand across his face. "Hardly the sophisticated criminal Aidan said he was, although cocky criminals often make stupid mistakes. After a flurry of activity on the account, they set up a sting, with the co-operation of the bank, but two weeks ago it all went quiet. That, maybe, coincides with when he was killed."

"What is it with these people?"

"What people?"

"Scammers, fraudsters," Fabia said angrily.

"Same as with any criminal, I suppose, when their criminality isn't caused by abject poverty. With people like Geddings, they come first, every other consideration trails way behind."

"I suppose. When I was in the force it wasn't nearly as bad, fraud of this kind, but it's increased by almost thirty percent in the last few years."

"How do you know that?" Matt asked without thinking.

"I keep myself informed, Matt," Fabia snapped. "I'm not completely cut off from the outside world, you know. My brain still works in spite of being a mother."

"Of course it does," Matt said quickly. "It's just that I wondered – you know – where you'd found that figure. Because it's absolutely right. The NFIB chap was talking about it."

"What I do, strangely enough," Fabia said, still sounding offended, "is read the papers and listen to the radio, and some podcasts. Just because I'm at home with Bethan a lot doesn't mean I'm brain-dead."

"Far from it," Matt said, then stretched out a hand and clasped hers. "Sorry. I was tactless. You're a saint and I'm a shit." He gave a twisted grin.

Fabia smiled back, but it was a bit forced. "Let's forget it," she said.

* * *

Fabia had just fallen asleep when her mobile pinged. She groaned and rolled over onto her elbow, and squinted at the illuminated numbers on her bedside clock. A quarter to twelve. Who could it be at this time of night? She was used to texts coming through at all hours on Matt's phone, but no longer on hers. She picked the mobile up and glanced at the screen. It was Cath. What on earth?

She pressed the yellow envelope icon and looked at the message.

> So sorry to disturb you. Huw is here and won't leave. I'm scared. Can Matt come?

Fabia knew that Cath would not have disturbed them if she could possibly have avoided it. This was serious. There was no point in asking her for an explanation. She just tapped in:

> Hang on. He'll be there soon.

Beside her, Matt stirred and muttered, "What's up? Is she awake?"

"It's not Bethan, it's Cath." She passed him her mobile and he squinted at the screen, reading the two messages. "Oh hell," he said as he swung his legs out of the bed. "You thought something like this might happen."

"I know. I'd go, but she specifically asks for you, and one of us has to stay with Bethan."

"It's okay. Don't worry." He pulled on his clothes, pushed a hand through his hair, and bent to kiss Fabia. "I'll try to make it quick."

She listened as his footsteps retreated down the stairs, then lay back under the duvet, knowing she wouldn't be able to go back to sleep anytime soon.

## Chapter 12

It was cold out and Matt decided to take the car. The vicarage was only ten minutes' walk away but he wanted to get there as soon as possible. He parked in the street rather than on the short driveway. Best be as quiet as possible. He hoped that the front door, under its triangular tiled porch, had been left unlocked, but it hadn't. Never mind. He knew Cath always left a key hidden in a particular spot in the flower bed beside the porch. Using his phone to light the way, he rummaged for it, found it, and unlocked the door.

Stepping into the tiled hallway, he heard voices coming from Cath's kitchen. Making his way down the hall as quietly as he could, he stopped just outside the door and listened.

"I know women, you see," said a man's voice. "You aren't any different just because you're wearing that dog collar."

"Wearing this collar signifies my marriage, so to speak, to the church. Now, please leave."

"No." The tone was more aggressive now. "I'm in love with you and I know you care about me."

"But only as your vicar, Huw. I do not care for you in any other way," Cath said, sounding desperate.

"Yes, you do." Matt could tell that Huw was smiling as he said this. "You've shown it in so many ways."

Matt wondered if he should leave it any longer before intervening. The next moment, he heard a crash and then Cath shouted, "Get out! Leave, now!"

No longer wondering, Matt pushed the kitchen door open.

Cath was standing up against the sink and a short stocky man with a balding head and a well-waxed moustache stood by the kitchen table. A broken mug lay on the floor between them. They both swung round as Matt came into the room.

"Hallo, Cath," Matt said quietly. "Having trouble?"

"Oh, thank God," Cath said. She came quickly over to Matt who put an arm round her shoulders.

"I got your message," Matt told her quietly.

"Who are you?" Huw, red in the face and blustering, went on, "Don't you know it's bloody rude to barge in on a private conversation?"

"To answer your first question, I'm a close friend of Cath's," Matt said, his tone icy. "My name is Matt Lambert, Chief Inspector Matt Lambert to be precise."

Matt could see the man's face pale a little and, for a split second, there was fear in his eyes, but it didn't last. There was still some fight in him.

"Do you make a habit of visiting Cath at this time of night?" Huw demanded.

"Not as a general rule," Matt said calmly, "but I could ask you the same question."

"Mine is a social call, Cath wants–"

"No, it is *not*," Cath cried. "You arrived on my doorstep at eleven o'clock at night with some excuse about needing advice. That's why I let you in. It's my duty to help my parishioners. Then you start– start telling me you want to stay, you want to take me to bed, and you refused to go when I asked you to, several times, I– I…" Cath came to a faltering stop and slumped down on a kitchen chair.

Matt walked towards Huw. He towered over the smaller man. "Is this true?" Matt asked, his voice quietly menacing.

"No, well, yes. But I knew that she didn't really mean it. It's just the way women are. They try to put you off but really, deep down, they want you to do the opposite of what they say. We men all know they want us to be strong and assertive, don't we?" He gave Matt a sickly smile and actually winked at him.

Matt could have thumped him then and there, but all he said was, "No, we don't. That's complete and utter nonsense."

Huw's face reddened again, and he straightened as if he was trying to stretch in order to seem taller, but Matt was still a head above him.

Huw took a step forward. "I suggest you leave, rather than me," he said.

"No!" Cath exclaimed.

Matt was tired and longing for his bed and this man was annoying him intensely. He was also aware that stalkers – and that was what Huw was – needed careful handling. He didn't want to push Huw into more extreme behaviour. That wouldn't help Cath at all.

"Cath texted and asked me to come around because you wouldn't leave," he said quietly. "She doesn't want you here, and I want to get back to my bed. I suggest you apologise for upsetting her and leave now, as I will, once I've made sure that you're gone."

"No, why should–"

Matt didn't let him get any further. "Alternatively," he said, his tone hardening, "we could make this official. I could call in with a couple of officers from uniform branch and they would escort you off the premises. That would probably entail them cautioning you, which would go on the record. It's up to you."

There was a silent stand-off between the two men as Cath looked on, frowning and anxious. Then Huw straightened his jacket and walked towards the kitchen door.

"If you insist, I will leave now. But this isn't the end of it." He looked across at Cath. "I'm sure you wouldn't behave like this if your friend had not interfered. I will see you at church on Sunday."

He turned to go and was about to close the kitchen door when Matt followed him out. Before Huw had the chance to open the front door, Matt barred his way.

"I am inclined to make this warning official, and if you pester Cath again, I will certainly do so. Is that understood?"

"I've met pipsqueaks like you when I was in the army, throwing their weight around, thinking–"

"That is *enough*," Matt said. "I will make a point of coming to see you in the next couple of days in my capacity as a chief inspector of police. Now go."

Matt pulled the front door open wide and stood waiting for the man to leave. Huw stared up at him, opened his mouth to speak, but something in Matt's face must have got through to him. He turned and walked rapidly down the driveway. Matt watched him go, then closed the door and returned to the kitchen.

Cath was still sitting at the table, her elbows on the polished pine, her head in her hands. She looked up as Matt came in.

"Thank you so much, Matt. I don't know what I would have done if you hadn't come round." Tears were glistening in her eyes. "I'm so, so sorry to have dragged you out, but I didn't know what else to do."

"No problem," Matt said, smiling at her. He was very fond of Fabia's best friend. "Fabia said something about the dean being in charge of pastoral care for the clergy. Have you contacted him about that puffed-up idiot?"

"Yes, but only briefly. He's not the most proactive person and he wasn't all that helpful, just said to let him know if I had any more trouble."

"Well, you have had," Matt said firmly. "I suppose you're in a bit of a cleft stick, Cath, what with him having an official role when it comes to parish affairs. Is he on the parish council as well as being a sidesman?"

Cath was relieved that, with Matt's background as the son and brother of clergymen, she didn't have to explain the workings of the parish to him. "No, thank goodness."

She pushed herself wearily from her chair and reached up to give Matt a hug. "You must get home, Matt, and I'm sorry, again, that I dragged you out. Go on, I'll be fine."

"Are you sure?"

"Absolutely. Go home and get some sleep."

As Matt got to the door, he said, "I'm sure Fabia will phone you tomorrow for an update, and I've told that stupid man that I'll be calling on him in an official – well, probably semi-official – capacity in the next couple of days. Do you know his address and phone number?"

"Yes, they're on the church records. I'll text them to you."

"Do you want to press charges against him? You are quite within your rights to do so."

Cath sighed. "No, please don't arrest him. I'm sure this will be enough of a warning to him. I'd be surprised if he tries it again."

"If you're sure. I'll outline the difference between being a friend and colleague and being a pain in the arse. I hope that'll do the trick."

Cath gave him a smile, but he could see that it was a bit forced. "I'm sure it will," she said.

"And about leaving that key in the flower bed, I suggest you don't do that anymore." He handed her the key.

"You're right, of course, but it bloody annoys me that I can't. This is Pontygwyn, not Newport or Cardiff."

"True," Matt said, "but things have changed, haven't they?"

Cath gave him a straight look. She knew what he meant. "Yes, over the last few years, I suppose they have."

# Chapter 13

Over an early breakfast the next morning, while Bethan bounced up and down in her high chair and stuffed her mouth with banana and raspberries, Matt brought Fabia up to date on what had happened at the vicarage.

"The whole situation rang alarm bells with me from the moment Cath told me about him," Fabia said. "I've been wracking my brains trying to work out why he seemed familiar, but I just can't place him."

"Maybe it's just that he's very much a type – ex-army, suffers from small-man syndrome, dresses like a country gent. It's almost a stereotype, a sort of Captain Mainwaring from *Dad's Army*."

"I know," Fabia said, frowning, "but I don't think it's that. Never mind. It'll come to me."

"I told him I'm going to see him in an official capacity in a couple of days' time. I hope that'll get through to him."

"Good," Fabia said as she cut up some squares of buttered toast and gave them to Bethan, who grabbed them and tried to stuff two into her mouth at once.

Matt grinned at his daughter. "You are a greedy little monster. You know that, don't you?" he said.

Bethan grinned at him through her mouthful of food.

"She's certainly a tidy eater, that's for sure," Fabia said, then she glanced at the kitchen clock. "It's half past seven, love, hadn't you better get going?"

"Yes, and if I have to stay late, I'll let you know."

"You do that," Fabia told him, "and text or WhatsApp me if there are any interesting developments."

"Will do."

Matt left the room and Fabia heard the front door close just as Bethan began to grizzle. She wiped her face clean of the remains of breakfast.

"Are your new teeth hurting you, *cariad*?" she cooed. "How about going out for a ride in the car? You like the car, don't you?"

Fabia pulled out her mobile and tapped in a number she hadn't used in years, not really surprised when the call didn't connect. No matter. She used to be a detective, and a good one at that. How hard could it be to find who she wanted to speak with?

She lifted Bethan out of the high chair, wrapped her up in her thick coat, then carried her out to the car. When Fabia was sure her daughter was safe and secure, she got behind the wheel and started the engine.

* * *

Half an hour later, just as Matt sat at the desk in his office, several things happened in quick succession, all needing his attention. First, Aidan came in with the promised spreadsheet of all the activity on Seth Geddings' computer and laptop, and more information he'd managed to extract from the SIM cards.

"I thought you'd be interested to know, sir," Aidan told him, "that all activity ceased on all his devices round about the same time. There's nothing on any of them since the 16th February. Each SIM card applies to an individual target and some of the activity on those stops earlier than that date. Not one of them has any recorded activity after that date."

"It looks as if that pins down when Geddings was killed, more or less," Matt said.

"Certainly does," Aidan said with satisfaction.

They were interrupted by Sara Gupta. "I've got the names of the two girls who overdosed, and a record of the action taken at the time. They were Casey and Carys Saunders, twins of seventeen, and their mother was living over by Belle Vue Park. No father in evidence. Do you want me to talk to the mam?"

"Not at the moment, Sara," Matt said. "We'll hold off for now, but thanks for the information."

Sara was followed by Dilys. "I've had a call from PC Heath from Swansea Central, sir. They informed Lois Clarke, Geddings' sister, that his body was found. She confirmed his identity but said she hadn't had any contact with him for over a year. Apparently, their mother and father both died within weeks of each other two years ago, and she blames that on her brother's behaviour."

"How come?" asked Matt.

"You know Mrs Cheng mentioned that he'd fallen out with his family," Dilys said. "Well, Geddings' sister told PC Heath that happened five years ago when he dropped out of uni – he was at the Pontypridd campus studying computer science. He moved out just after. She says both parents had health problems, but she feels that his behaviour precipitated their deaths. I've asked Heath to send me a transcript of the interview with Lois Clarke. It should come through any minute."

"Good work, Dilys. Bring it to me directly you get it."

The three of them went back to their desks, but Dilys returned ten minutes later.

"Here's the transcript, sir."

Matt started reading through it and Dilys sat down to wait.

After a few minutes had ticked by, Matt looked up at her and said, "This bit here about her bumping into someone who told her they'd seen her brother in Usk. How long ago was that? It's not clear."

"I think she met this person quite recently, but she was told that they'd seen her brother a few months before," Dilys told him. "Do you want me to double-check with Sergeant Heath?"

"Please do."

Another ten minutes went by then Dilys was back. "She says it was about six months ago. It was an old school friend of them both – a woman. Lois gave no name, but she said this person called out to Seth, but he didn't hear her, or didn't want to talk to her, perhaps."

The next person needing Matt's attention was Karen Johns, who walked in with some further information. "I think I've got something for you," she told Matt. "We had a DNA test done on some hairs found at Geddings' rooms, some found on his body, and some found on Seddon's clothing. They were all dark hairs – unlike the victims' – and all from the same person. I've checked with the database and they're not on record, so whoever they belong to hasn't been convicted of a crime within the last five years."

"But it still helps. At least it confirms this person was present at both sites and could be responsible. It means we can dovetail the two investigations to a certain extent. I'll get one of my team to do some further in-depth research into the two victims' backgrounds. What can you tell me about the old steam vent discovered in the Usk tunnel?"

"Not much, I'm afraid. Dr Curtis agreed the body was posted through it and that the drop shattered the victim's legs. I had a good look at the area surrounding the vent, but the ground was very cut up. No tyre marks from a vehicle but plenty smaller tyre impressions – mountain bikes probably – and even some hoof prints." She smiled. "I'm sure that if Seddon had been tied to the saddle of a horse to move him, someone would have noticed."

"Yes, I agree. Thanks for checking though."

Karen nodded and left the office.

Before the interruptions, Matt had been going over and over the information they'd gleaned so far. He sent the chief superintendent an e-mail outlining their progress. Progress, he thought ruefully, not much of that at the moment.

At nine, Sara Gupta knocked on his door and came in. "I've done that research, sir. I haven't had time to write it up yet, but I thought you might like to see some of the notes I've made."

"I would indeed," Matt said. "Take a seat."

"I started with the first victim, at least, he was the first one found: Jake Seddon. He trained as a pharmacist at Anglia Ruskin University in Cambridge, then returned to Wales and settled in Bridgend. That was in 2006. He married the following year. His wife's maiden name was Gwyneth Michaelson, her father was the younger brother of Dai and Paul Michaelson's father. It seems that Seddon first worked in a perfectly legit pharmacy in Tondu, but he was sacked. I found a newspaper report about him being fined for selling antibiotics and anti-depressants without a prescription, which was why they gave him the push. That was in 2010. After that, he seemed to drop off the radar for a bit, but reappeared when he was investigated for manufacturing methamphetamines. There was an anonymous tip-off but, as we know, they couldn't make the charge stick."

"I think that's when Fabia came across him," Matt said.

"Yes. I read through a transcript of the interview by Chief Inspector – as she was then – Havard and Sergeant Gwyn Jones. They certainly put him through the wringer, particularly Sergeant Jones, but in the end they had to let him go."

"Anything else?" Matt asked. "I believe Fabia interviewed Seddon again when those twins died of an overdose."

"Yes. I read through that transcript as well, but that too came to nothing. I did come across a report that there'd been a raid on some units on Thorn Road industrial estate. An anonymous tip-off again."

"I wonder who it is that tried to get him arrested," Matt said.

"I'm afraid I don't know but I can check the calls," Sara said with enthusiasm. "They would have been recorded."

"Good idea."

"The second tip-off told them there was an industrial unit being used as a laboratory to manufacture drugs. The unit in question was owned by the Michaelson brothers, but when the drug squad got there, it was empty, clean as a whistle. They did find minute traces of chemicals, but nothing they could hang a hat on."

"All very frustrating," Matt said and rubbed his eyes. "I know this happened a while ago, but we'd better request another search of that unit, just to be sure. I'll organise a warrant. How about Seth Geddings? Did you find out anything useful about him?"

"Not much more than we knew already, sir," Sara said regretfully. "I found no connection between him and Seddon, except that they both lived in this area. He had a couple of speeding fines but the most interesting thing was…" Sara looked at her laptop screen and ran a finger over the mouse pad for a moment. "Here it is," she said. "He was suspected of hacking into several small business computer systems, with a view to blackmail. The investigating officers got so far as sending the case to the CPS, but it never came to trial. That was seven years ago. He was living in Swansea at the time."

"That all adds a bit of background to both," Matt said, trying to keep the disappointment out of his voice. "This whole business has seemed to turn up case after case that never came to anything. Keep digging and let me know what you find out from those recordings." Matt got to his feet and took his coat from the rack. "We'll catch up first thing tomorrow."

* * *

Matt drove back to Pontygwyn, pulled up outside the house and yawned. He didn't feel he was being much use to Fabia lately and missed spending time with Bethan before she went to bed. He got out of the car, walked up to the front door and let himself in.

"I'm home," he called.

"We're in the kitchen," Fabia called.

He walked along the hall to the rear of the house. She looked up and smiled. He wrapped his arm around her, kissed her firmly then turned his attention to Bethan, who was dozing in her car seat.

"Have you been somewhere today?" he asked.

"We have, we went for a drive to the seaside."

"Isn't it a bit cold for that? Anyway, I thought we'd take her to the beach together when she's a little older and the weather warms up."

"We didn't go to the beach. We went for a cuppa with Gwyn Jones."

"You did what?" Matt asked, angrily.

"I told you, we popped in on Gwyn Jones."

"And you took Bethan with you?"

"Glenys Pritchard couldn't take her at such short notice and I couldn't leave her, so yes, I took her with me. You know how she loves the car." Fabia turned away from the sink and put her hands on her hips. "I don't see what's wrong with that. Gwyn is an ex-colleague. I worked with him."

Matt dragged his hand down his face and groaned. "You didn't tell me you were planning to visit him."

"So now I have to tell you where I am all the time, do I?"

"I'm not saying that–"

"What are you saying then?"

Matt paused. "I worry about you, both of you."

"There's no need." Fabia turned back to the sink to finish the washing up. Without looking at him, she said, "It isn't like we didn't talk about me contacting him."

"You're right, of course, but if I remember correctly, I said you shouldn't and that you should leave it to me."

Fabia emptied the washing-up bowl, dried her hands on a towel and sat at the table.

"I just it thought it would help," she said. "You've been so busy with the murder investigations, and coming home so late, tired and stressed."

"Which is why I'm being snippy. Sorry." Matt reached across the table and took Fabia's hand. "So, tell me then, what did Gwyn Jones have to say?"

"He was very pleased to see us and had a lot to say, but I'm not sure anything he said will help you."

"How did he end up in Mumbles?"

"As you know, he took early retirement."

"Was he forced into that?" Matt asked.

"Not at all. He wasn't enjoying the desk job so when his mother died and left him enough money that he didn't need to work, he packed it in, upped sticks and bought a lovely house with a pretty garden." Fabia smiled. "As I said, he was pleased to see us and made such a fuss of our little chick."

"Did he say anything about Seddon?"

"Only that he was disgusted we couldn't make anything stick and the man was allowed to walk. He heard about the death of the twins and was certain Seddon made the drugs that killed them. He was pretty angry about that."

"Angry enough to seek vengeance?"

Fabia laughed. "I'm not sure Gwyn was ever into vengeance, but I guess people can change… under the right circumstances."

# Chapter 14

While the double murder investigation continued to crawl along, Fabia had problems of her own. On Thursday morning, at a meeting of the LSCB, George Morris, the probation officer on the board, had questioned almost every suggestion she made. It was clear he had no respect for her as their chairperson. They had been discussing a family he'd had dealings with and by the end of the meeting, Fabia could tell that his attitude was bothering the other members too, particularly Chloe Daniels. Fabia had decided she would have to challenge his behaviour, but wanted to wait until the others had gone. She was lucky that the other members were quick to leave and, as George got up to follow them, Fabia saw her chance.

"Could you hang on a minute, George?" she said quietly.

He turned but didn't come further into the room. Fabia walked across and closed the door firmly, then said, "Please, take a seat."

George pulled out the nearest chair and sat down. "I've got another meeting in–" he glanced at his watch "–half an hour. What can I do for you?"

Fabia took a seat opposite him and rested her arms on the table, hands clasped. "I get the strong impression that you find me difficult to work with," she said in her direct way. "Am I right?"

He frowned and his skin reddened under his short greying beard. "I don't know what– I wouldn't say difficult, but you must admit, we have had our moments in the past."

"You're thinking of what, precisely?" Fabia asked, eyebrows raised.

"I– er– found some of your methods somewhat difficult to deal with." He stirred on the chair as if he was physically uncomfortable.

"Can you give me an example?"

"There were times when I felt you pushed too hard with people who were vulnerable."

Fabia felt anger rise up inside her, but she clamped it down. She'd always thought she was fair and empathetic, and this made her feel she'd been wrong about herself. Wrong, at least, about how she came across. "Are you thinking of anyone in particular? I'd like to know so that I can get a better idea of what you mean."

"There was one case, a young lad from that estate in Cwmbran who was a bit of an arsonist, very tricky family background, very vulnerable. Trevor Davis, his name was. It was just before you went on your so-called… your, er– your sick leave."

His hesitation was not lost on Fabia, and the term 'so-called' stung. She took a deep breath. She'd come across this attitude before but had hoped not to do so again. She gave him a sharp look, but he wouldn't look her in the eye.

"I felt you were very hard on him," he added, "pursued him in fact."

"Isn't that what police officers do when dealing with a criminal?" Fabia could have kicked herself. That sounded so pompous, and also as if she was making excuses.

"But there are limits. Still," he added, "I'm sure you were under a lot of strain at the time. You were, no doubt, not at your best."

Patronising or what? Fabia thought. She clamped her teeth together in an effort to control her temper. This wasn't getting them anywhere.

"I don't think I allowed my personal problems to affect my job, and they certainly won't now – should I have any problems, that is." She got up and hitched her bag on to her shoulder. "You're obviously aware of the fact that my name was cleared after that debacle over the contaminated land, and that the appropriate people were prosecuted?" It was a question, not a statement. Fabia waited for him to respond.

"Yes. I did hear something of the sort."

Of course, you did, you stupid man, Fabia thought. "I wouldn't be here now if my name had not been cleared," she said. "Perhaps it would be a good idea if you asked Chief Superintendent Talbot to reassure you about my capabilities and my past. She knows exactly what happened, and I'm sure she consulted you all before appointing me."

He didn't say anything in response to this.

"Let's try and work together from now on, George. After all, it's the children and their families who matter here, not our personal feelings."

He nodded. "Of course."

Fabia didn't think there was any 'of course' about it. She was pretty sure he would continue to be a bit of a thorn in her side.

"You'd better get on to that meeting of yours," she said coolly and, without saying anything more, she opened the door and left the room.

Damn, damn, damn, she thought, that did not go well.

It had been over four years now since she'd been cleared of corruption, for goodness sake. When would the past stop rearing its ugly head? But then, returning to work in this building, wasn't that asking for the past to intrude? It had been here that she'd been accused, here that the whispers and the furtive glances had haunted her. And here that she'd been ordered to take sick leave while her supposed misdemeanours were investigated. As she came out into reception, she looked down a corridor to her right. Down there was one of the secure interrogation rooms she had often used. A sudden flashback took her completely by surprise. Her eyes widened and she stopped in her tracks. A moment later, she turned on her heel and went back up the stairs. She must tell Matt about this.

* * *

Several people looked up as Fabia made her way through the main office. Dilys smiled. "Hiya, Fabia, how's tricks? Are you looking for the chief inspector?"

"Yes, I am. I've got something useful to tell him."

"I'm sure it'll be fine if you go straight through."

Feeling a bit silly for doing so, Fabia knocked on Matt's door. When she went in, she found him slumped in his chair gazing at the computer screen. He looked up and smiled.

"Meeting over?"

"Yes," she said, going around the desk to give him a quick kiss.

"How did it go?" Matt asked.

He didn't sound quite so strained about it this morning. Good, thought Fabia.

"Not too bad, although I had to have a word with George Morris. He's proper contrary. If I simply said it's a nice day, I think he'd argue. But that's not what I've come to tell you. It's something that might be useful when it comes to helping Cath."

"Oh?" said Matt, not sounding exactly bowled over by this.

Fabia sat down opposite his desk. "Listen. I had this flash of, well, déjà vu I suppose. I can pin it down to a particular time as it was just after I moved to the Gwent force. We had that awful murder case, the Llewellyn brothers who killed their elderly parents. I remember having them in, one after the other, and I'd nearly got one of them to talk when I was told to leave it to someone else. It was so frustrating. That's why I remember it."

"What has that got to do with Cath?"

"The case I was moved to was out of the area. I had to go over Carmarthen way to interrogate this bloke who was stalking some poor woman who lived in Pontypool. She committed suicide because of it. At least, that was what her suicide note said. I remember her name because it was unusual. Sky Laska. I'm sure we'd be able to search out the records on the case."

"Okay, but I still don't get it."

"Sorry. It's just that I'm sure the man I interviewed was Huw Prosser, except that wasn't the name he was going by then. What was it?" Fabia closed her eyes in an effort to remember, then slapped a hand to her knee and pointed a triumphant finger at Matt. "Harry Pierce, that's what it was. Strange how people who change their name often stick to the same initials."

"What do you want me to do about it, Fabia?" Matt said.

There was silence in the room for a few moments, then Fabia sagged a little. "I know how busy you are, but perhaps one of your team could check on the records, get some info on this Huw Prosser – or Harry Pierce – character. Then I could face him with it. That might make him leave Cath alone. Please, Matt."

"Won't he recognise you? You're pretty distinctive."

"Thank you, kind sir," Fabia said, taking this as a compliment. "I don't think he will. I was in uniform then, with my hair pulled into that awful bun I used to wear. Anyway, would it matter if he did?"

Matt pulled at an earlobe as he gazed across his desk at Fabia, then shrugged. "Okay, just for you. But be careful, my love. I don't want him turning his attention to you. On second thoughts, I'll go and tackle him. I told him I'd be coming round to have a word.

"Good," Fabia said. She got up and slipped behind the desk to plant a kiss on his cheek. "You are a treasure."

"And you are a crafty woman," Matt said, putting his arm round her as they went to the door.

She grinned and blew him a kiss, hearing him call out for DC Becca Pryce as she went.

# Chapter 15

All the arrangements had been made with Mrs Pritchard's daughter, Glenys, and Bethan was spending her second day with her child-minder. When Fabia collected her from the neat little house in Church Road, she decided to go on up to the vicarage and pop in on Cath. She glanced at the dashboard clock as she started up the car and saw that it was half past three. At this time of day, she'd a good chance of finding her friend at home.

A few minutes later, she parked in the vicarage driveway. She reached in to get Bethan out of her car seat but straightened up again when she heard the front door of the vicarage slam. She turned to see if it was Cath, but it wasn't. It was Huw Prosser. He took no notice of her and Bethan. Fabia didn't even know if he saw them as he walked rapidly across the vicarage garden. A moment later, he marched across Church Road into The Oaks pub car park.

"Let me get you out of there quick," Fabia said to her daughter. "I think your Auntie Cath might have a problem."

Fabia didn't bother with the front door but, hefting Bethan onto her hip, she hurried around the side of the house to the door into the kitchen. It was open.

She stepped in. "Cath," she called, "it's me. Are you okay?"

Fabia went through to the hall and Cath came out of her study at the same time. Fabia gasped. Cath looked terrible. Her curly hair was in a mess and her clothes had obviously been pulled about. She was white as a sheet except for a dark red patch which stood out on her cheek, and there was a cut on her lip. It looked as if she'd been hit.

"Oh, my dear," Fabia said, "what has happened to you?" She went to her friend, put her free arm around her and led her back into the kitchen.

"Sit. Here, take Bethan," Fabia said. "I'll put the kettle on and make some tea, then you can tell me all about it. I suppose it was that bloody man again. I saw him leaving."

"Yes," Cath said. She tried to smile at Bethan who was trying to grasp the cross and chain she wore round her neck. "I… I… oh God!"

"Hang on. Let me get this tea made."

Thinking that Bethan's warm little body would help Cath more than most things at the moment, she said no more as she went about putting teabags into mugs and getting the milk out of the fridge. As she did so, she kept an eye on Cath who was giving Bethan a smile now. That was a good sign. Cath kept some toys for the parish children who visited the vicarage, and Fabia dragged the box out from beside one of the cupboards. She took Bethan from Cath's lap, put her down on a rug and took out a few toys for her to play with. Only then did she put the mug of tea in front of Cath.

Fabia sat down opposite her with her hands clasped round her own mug. "Tell me. What did he do?"

"He said he'd come to apologise for his behaviour the other night. I couldn't very well not let him do so."

"Oka-ay," Fabia said, without further comment. There was no point in telling Cath she shouldn't have given him the chance.

"The thing is, he came in the back way, through here. He's never done that before. He was in the room before I even realised. I thought, if we went through to the study, sort of treated it like church business, he would behave." She gave a shuddering sigh. "I was wrong."

"What did he do?" Fabia asked as she bent to give Bethan another toy. Thank goodness for a placid child, she thought.

"It was okay to begin with. He was doing all this apologising and saying that he'd meant me no harm and stuff, but all the time he was talking, I could see in his eyes that he didn't mean any of it. Then he started on that ridiculous 'when women say no, they really mean yes' business. I'm afraid I rather lost my temper at that point."

"I'm not surprised."

"It deteriorated from there. It's hard to remember exactly what happened. I know he grabbed me, and I lashed out, but he caught my wrist." Cath took in a shuddering breath and pulled up her sleeve to reveal red marks on her fair skin.

"Did he hit you, Cath?" Fabia asked gently.

"Yes. He said I was getting hysterical. He slapped me hard across the face."

"Bastard!" Fabia exclaimed. Bethan looked up anxiously from the rug and Fabia picked her up. "Sorry, pet, didn't mean to scare you." She turned back to Cath. "You really have to report this to the police, Cath. Not necessarily Matt, although he did say he was going to go and give Huw a talking to. If Matt's too busy, I– we could ask Dilys to visit him. She takes no prisoners when it comes to shits like Huw. I'll give her a ring now. What do you think?"

Cath chewed at her lip, her eyes big and anxious, then she sagged a little. "I suppose it has to be done. I can't go on like this."

"That's my girl." Fabia gave her a straight look. "Are you willing to press charges?"

"I don't know. Do you think I should?

"Yes, he assaulted you, end of," Fabia said firmly. "Quite apart from anything else, even if you didn't, the police could take it into their own hands and go ahead anyway."

Fabia took her mobile from the pocket of her jacket and keyed in the number. When Dilys picked up, Fabia quickly explained what had happened.

"What a shit!" Dilys exclaimed. "I'll enjoy dealing with him, but I won't be able to go right now, Fabia."

"I didn't think you would. I know how busy you all are."

"I promise I'll go around later, as soon as possible. I'll probably take Craig with me just in case the stupid man gets antsy. I'll speak to the chief first, though."

"Absolutely. I don't want you getting into trouble with Matt, or me for that matter. He does get a bit shirty if I interfere too much."

Fabia heard a gurgle of laughter from Dilys. "Never to God, Fabia. Anyway, leave it with me."

"You're a gem, Dilys. Matt has his address, by the way."

"Okay, and give my best to the vicar. She's alright, she is."

## Chapter 16

Dilys and Craig arrived at the address Matt had given them, a neat semi-detached house in Cobett Avenue, at half past six that evening. They parked easily enough a few yards from the front door and walked along to number eight. A dark-red Range Rover was parked in the paved area in front of the house and Dilys turned to Craig. "Good sign. He should be in if his car is here."

But when they got to the porch and she rang the bell, there was no response.

"Sarge," Craig said, "this door isn't completely closed."

"You're right," Dilys said. She gave it a push and it slowly swung open. "Mr Prosser?" she called, but there was no reply. "Mr Prosser?" she called again.

Nothing.

Frowning, with a hand held out to stop Craig going any further, she looked all around the hall. On the left-hand side, the stairs rose up to the floor above. There was a half-moon-shaped table to the right. A polished wooden bowl on it held various keys, a few AA batteries and some elastic bands. The usual sort of odds and ends, Dilys thought. The passageway directly opposite them led to a door at the back, probably the kitchen, and there was another door halfway down on their right. Both doors were closed.

"I don't like the feel of this," Dilys said. "Go round the back, Craig, and have a look through the windows, then come back and tell me what you find. I'll stay here."

It wasn't long before Craig was back. "I looked through the kitchen window. There's a light on in there but no one about. It looks as if there's been some kind of confrontation – chairs knocked over, a couple of mugs smashed on the floor."

"Okay. Let me just call the chief and ask what he wants us to do."

When Dilys got through to Matt, she explained what they'd found.

"Are you sure there's no one there?" he asked.

"Not entirely, but–"

At that moment, they were interrupted by a woman in the next-door house coming out of her front door. She was small, elderly and wearing a floral apron which she was smoothing down. Her bright eyes studied them, full of curiosity.

"Are you looking for Mr Prosser?" she asked.

"Hang on, sir," Dilys said to Matt, then turned to the woman. "Yes, do you know where he is?"

"I heard a bit of a noise about an hour ago, so I looked out my front window by there," she said. "After a moment, I saw Mr Prosser and another man come out and get into a car and drive off, but it did seem a bit strange."

"How do you mean?"

"Well, they didn't close Mr Prosser's door properly, and they were moving really fast. It was as if the other man was pushing Mr Prosser. He got into the back of the car, not the front. It was a black car, like one of those taxis they have in London."

"Thank you, madam. Would it be alright if we came to speak to you once we've had a look around?"

"I don't know how helpful I can be, but I'm in all evening. I don't like going out after dark."

"We'll be round now in a minute." Dilys turned back to her phone. "Sir, are you still there?"

"Yes, what's up?"

Dilys explained what she'd just learned. "We're going to have a nosey, then go round and have a word with the witness."

"Okay," Matt said. "I'll wait to hear from you."

"Yes, sir."

She relayed this information to Craig. "Go back to the car and get the kit out, Craig, and we'll have a look around."

When he came back, they both pulled on latex gloves and put disposable overshoes on, then stepped into the hallway. First, they made their way to the kitchen and Dilys carefully opened the door, trying to put as little pressure on the handle as possible. It was just as Craig had described. The room was rather bare, with a minimal amount of equipment on the work surfaces, just a kettle and a toaster in evidence, and a mug tree on its side. Three mugs had scattered, unbroken. Two had fallen to the floor and smashed. There was nothing on the windowsill and there were no pictures on the walls. Two kitchen chairs lay on their sides.

Craig had followed Dilys into the room. "Sarge, look at this," he said, pointing at a tall fridge-freezer.

The doors were covered in photos. Some were attached by magnets and some taped to the door. Every single one was of the same person: Cath Temple. There were photos of her in full vestments, of her in casual clothes, some taken of her greeting people at the church door, some of her walking along the High Street in Pontygwyn or through the graveyard next to the church, and a couple of her in The Oaks pub, looking relaxed with a group of friends.

"Good God," Dilys said softly. "Well, there can be no doubt about Mr Prosser hounding the vicar. This rather adds to it, doesn't it?"

"It certainly does," Craig said, sounding disgusted.

They both stood still and looked carefully around the rest of the room. There was nothing else of note. What to do? Dilys could tell that something untoward had happened, but they needed more information. Would Prosser be back any minute, or would he be gone for hours? She decided to call Matt again and ask what he thought was best to do.

"Go next door and speak to the neighbour, get more details," he told her. "We can't spend too much time on this with two murders to investigate, so get back here as soon as you can."

When Dilys knocked on the neighbour's door, it was answered before she even lowered her hand. They were led into a cluttered room full of photos, china and glass knick-knacks. Several cushions had brightly crocheted covers and there was a fur rug in front of the artificial coal fire. Both Dilys and Craig showed their warrant cards as they were urged to sit.

"I should tell you my name," the elderly woman said. "I'm Ena Williams, Mrs Ena Williams. I've been living y'ere, oh, there's years, and I know all my neighbours. What do you want to ask me?" She gave them a bright eager smile.

"How well do you know Mr Prosser?" asked Dilys.

"Not that well, I have to admit," she said regretfully. "He's only been next door since the Barkers moved, they had to go into sheltered housing, see. That was about three years ago, give or take."

"Is he a good neighbour?"

"I've no complaints. He keeps himself to himself. He told me he goes to St Cybi's, while I'm chapel, so we don't meet up that much."

"Can you tell us what you heard this morning?"

"Well" – she leant forward in her chair – "I was doing my front window, I do like clean windows, and I saw this black car park just by there." She waved a hand in the direction of the front of the house. "The trouble is my phone rang. It was my daughter, Melody, she always phones of an evening, so I didn't see the driver get out. It was just as I put the phone down that I heard this banging next door, and shouting. I couldn't hear the words, exactly, although I think someone shouted, 'How dare you?' After that, it went quiet for a bit, then I saw Mr Prosser come out of his front door with another man behind him and they got into the car, like I said. I saw it all because of the streetlight out there, and my porch light was on."

Dilys could tell that Craig wanted to join the conversation so she gave him a nod.

"What did the other man look like?" Craig asked.

"He was short but sort of powerful-looking, stocky, and he had a cap on, you know, like those ones that the youngsters wear back to front. I couldn't see what colour his hair was, but I got the impression he was probably youngish. He certainly moved quickly, not like an old man, see. Striding, he was."

"Would you say that Mr Prosser was going with him willingly?" asked Craig.

Mrs Williams' eyes widened. "Do you think he was being forced to go with that other man?"

"I really can't say," Craig said. "What do you think?"

"It didn't look right, somehow," she said with a frown. "I can't say exactly why. They were walking very quickly. Mr Prosser stumbled at one point and the other man grabbed his arm. No, it didn't seem right."

"Were they talking as they walked to the car?" Dilys asked.

"I don't think so. I didn't hear anything. The car was driven off so fast." She shook her head in disapproval. "People really shouldn't drive fast on a road like this. Lots of families with children live round here. What if some little kiddie had run across the road?"

"Did you happen to make a note of the registration of the car, Mrs Williams?" asked Dilys.

The elderly lady shook her head. "No, sorry, the car was parked on the street so I couldn't see it from here, and it was too quick to see when it drove off."

Dilys decided to wind up the interview as she thought they probably wouldn't get anything more from Mrs Williams. She smiled and rose from her chair. "Thank you very much for being so helpful," she said. "We'll leave you in peace now."

"Oh, alright, but if there's anything else I can do–"

"Of course, we'll get back to you."

Once they were back in their car, Dilys said to Craig, "All a bit of a mystery, but there isn't much we can do until Mr Prosser turns up again. We don't have enough to say he was taken against his will."

"I know," Craig said, frowning, "but I can't help thinking that there's something going on that we don't know about."

Dilys grinned at him. "There always is, Craig. It's the nature of the job. We just have to make sure we find out."

"I know. Still, I'd really like to have a word with this Prosser bloke."

"So would I. He's been a pain in the arse for the vicar and she doesn't deserve shit like that. I'll let uniform know we'd like a word and they should keep an eye out."

"She's always been good to me. Let's hope we find him sooner rather than later."

Neither of them knew that they'd be doing so very soon, but not quite in the way that Craig envisaged.

# Chapter 17

The call came in at half past ten the following morning. A body had been found half-buried in the muddy edge of the river Usk just below St Madoc Church in Llanbadoc. A man walking his dog had noticed a shoe protruding from the greenery that hung over the river and, on investigating, had discovered the body. Realising that the man was dead, he had the wit not to disturb the area any further and dialled 999.

On being told of the discovery, Matt's reaction was predictable. "Bloody hell! This is the third one around Pontygwyn and Usk in less than two weeks. What is going on round here?"

Dilys, who had brought him the news, had no answer to this question.

Matt tapped in Chief Superintendent Talbot's extension number and, when she picked up, told her what had been found. "I'll get the SOCO team deployed, ma'am, but I'll go as well. I want to check it all out and don't want to be alarmist, but I've a nasty feeling about this, given that it's the third body found in such a short time."

Once he'd ended the call, Matt pushed himself up from his chair, grabbed his coat and came around the desk.

"Right, Dilys, you're with me, and get Tom to organise uniform to make sure we keep the public at bay. Far too many people walk along the bank there, so we'll need plenty of personnel on site."

* * *

Matt and Dilys arrived not long after the SOCO van. Having kitted themselves out in the required white overalls, they stepped gingerly towards an area cordoned off with the ubiquitous blue and white crime scene tape. The ancient Church of St Madoc stood stoically, surrounded on three sides by gravestones, some ancient and leaning at an angle, some more recent. The grass was velvety amongst them. There was a steep slope in the land down to the river, so they had to step carefully.

The SOCO team had just finished setting up a white plastic enclosure to protect the remains and Karen Johns was standing talking to one of her team just outside it. She turned as they approached.

"Ah, Chief Inspector, this is becoming a bit of a habit."

"It is," Matt said, his tone sardonic. "Any idea yet of what we have?"

"We've hardly begun. It's a white male, probably middle-aged, but that's as much as I know so far."

"Is the chap who phoned in still here?"

"Yes. I asked him to wait as I thought you might want a word. He's over there, talking to DC Tom Watkins."

Matt looked around to see a dark-skinned young man standing with a cocker spaniel on a lead. The dog sat quietly beside him, occasionally giving his master an anxious look. Matt walked over and Tom introduced them.

"This is Mr Joseph who discovered the body," Tom said.

"Good morning, sir. Did you notice anyone else around at the time?" Matt asked.

"No. Just me and Dolly here." He indicated the dog. "It was her that found him. I realised he was dead. I'm a nurse at the Royal Gwent so I suppose I know the signs."

"Have you any idea who he is?" Matt asked, not holding out much hope.

"I'm afraid not. It was difficult to see all of the body. I decided it was best not to try to pull him out of the mud. I've seen enough TV detective dramas to know you mustn't contaminate the area."

Matt smiled in response to this. It wasn't the first time he'd heard that from a member of the public. "Thank you for your prompt action, sir. Perhaps you could give my colleague here your details in case we have to contact you again."

He left Mr Joseph with Tom and went back to the activity beside the river.

* * *

Two hours later, Matt and Dilys got back to the station. Karen Johns had given him a few details about the body and what she'd said had rung distinct alarm bells. They'd discussed the situation on the way back and had decided they must call a meeting of as many of the team as possible. This investigation needed to be pulled together and all the information pooled before they went any further. Tom arrived back within seconds of Matt and Dilys.

They all gathered in the main office, perched on desks, leaning against the wall or sitting at their computers. A whiteboard displayed all the relevant photographs of the first two crime scenes. They only had verbal information about the third victim so far, but at least they had a name, as Matt had been able to identify the man.

There was a hubbub of talk. Chloe Daniels slipped into the room just as Matt held up a hand for quiet. The noise died down to silence.

"Okay, people, let me recap on what we've got. Three murder victims. They were not killed where they were found. All three bodies had been transported, somehow, from the place where they were tortured and killed to where they were found. The first body discovered was Jake Seddon." Matt indicated the appropriate photo pinned to the board. "As you know, he was found in the Usk railway tunnel. We have determined he was dropped through an old steam vent, but not sure how he was taken there, or where he was killed. The body shows signs of torture before death. The SOCO team are sure he wasn't killed or tortured at his home address. The team in Bridgend made a comprehensive search and found nothing."

"Are they sure of that?" Dilys asked.

"It seems so. We have to take their word for it. Seddon was a pharmacist who was suspected of manufacturing illegal drugs and had come to our notice in the past, but released without charge. The second victim was Seth Geddings. He was a scammer who was leaching thousands from vulnerable victims and was being investigated by the NFIB. It looks as if he was tortured in his rooms above the garage where he lived. Only traces of blood were found, so he too was killed elsewhere."

Matt paced in front of the board, hands in his pockets. "Then there is the body found this morning; a man called Huw Prosser. Now, this one is slightly different in that he'd not come to our notice before, as far as we knew. I had occasion to speak to him on an informal basis as he was bothering – stalking – the Reverend Cath Temple from St Cybi's Church in Pontygwyn."

Matt paused, but no one interrupted. "In a bit of luck, Fabia Havard, ex-Superintendent in this station, recognised him as Harry Pierce who was questioned for stalking a woman in Pontypool several years ago. That woman, Sky Laska, committed suicide and suggested in her suicide note that he was responsible."

There was a low muttering, a mixture of disgust and pity, around the room.

"Aspects of the killings link all three deaths and convince me we're dealing with only one murderer," Matt said. "All three bodies show signs of having been cut on the chest with a very sharp object. The pathologist thinks that a Stanley knife was used. Not deep cuts but enough to cause plenty of bleeding. Here and here" – he pointed at photographs on the whiteboard – "you can see what was done to the first two. On both, it looks as if the perpetrator might have been trying to form letters. Marks found on Prosser are very similar. The other thing that links them is that they'd all had three fingers of their right hands broken." Matt looked around the room. "Any questions?"

"That was one of the Dai Michaelson's trademarks, wasn't it?" Tom Watkins asked. "Breaking fingers."

"It was," Matt said.

"Do you think someone's trying to frame him?"

"If that is the case, that person is not aware that Dai Michaelson is in prison," Matt pointed out.

"True," said Tom.

Sara Gupta spoke up. "Could Seddon's death be a case of revenge, sir? Those twins that died of an overdose, maybe a member of their family took things into their own hands."

"Possibly, Sara, but why kill the other two?"

"Perhaps to complicate things," Sara suggested, "to confuse us and make it more difficult for us to find the killer."

"That still doesn't really explain it. How would a member of their family have known about what the other two had got up to?"

Sara grimaced. "Um, I hadn't thought of that. Although, as far as I am aware, the only family member was the mother, no father on the scene but we should check that."

"Sir," Becca Pryce, sitting at her computer, put a hand up. "You asked me to do some research into Huw Prosser aka Harry Pierce. I've just had some information through from the Carmarthen records office. It confirms that he was accused of stalking and was let off with a caution. Apparently, the *South Wales Guardian* did a series of articles about the problems of stalking, one of which named him in connection with the suicide of Sky Laska, as Ms Havard suggested. He threatened to sue them, but that didn't happen and it wasn't long before he left the area. The press reported that he'd 'run away' as he'd refused to be interviewed by any of their reporters."

"Do they say where he went?"

"No," Becca said, "but obviously we know now. Strangely, I couldn't find any more details about him."

"Dilys and Craig spoke to Prosser's neighbour yesterday and she told them he'd gone off with someone in a black cab, like the London ones. We must find that cab, so I'd like you, Claire, to do a trawl of the taxi and car hire firms, find out if any of them have such a vehicle. Also track down any family he might have."

Claire nodded and jotted down some notes.

"Do you think the black cab is significant?" Dilys asked. "It has a larger space behind the driver's seat than other cars do and, to my mind, that would make it easier to get a body in and out of the car."

"That's a point," said Matt, "although we know Prosser was alive when he left his house with the other man. Tracing that individual is a priority."

There was a murmur of agreement around the room.

Matt nodded. "The SOCO team will be searching Prosser's house, but we'll have to wait for Karen Johns' report on that, which doesn't help us right this minute. We do know now that there is a tenuous link between all three of them: criminal activity that has gone unpunished. Drugs in Seddon's case, fraud in Geddings', and stalking in

Prosser's – all in and around this area – and their criminal activity was aimed at people rather than property."

"Do you think it could be someone like an investigative journalist who's become obsessed with them?" Chloe asked.

Matt frowned. "Always possible," he said, "but why kill them when you could write about them, and ruin their lives that way?"

"I suppose," said Chloe, "particularly if it was spread all over the tabloids and social media."

"We still have the possibility that Paul Michaelson is involved, but why?" Matt said.

"Some kind of family feud in the case of Jake Seddon, and Paul could have been copying his brother's nasty habits," Dilys suggested, "but that wouldn't explain the other two, unless Sara's right and it's an attempt to confuse us, although that seems a bit extreme."

Matt nodded in agreement. "I want you all to concentrate on the areas I've given you. Dilys and I will be going to speak to Reverend Temple to ask if she has any idea who could have killed Prosser."

"Do you think she was involved, sir?" asked Becca.

"I don't think so," Matt said. "One thing that stands out in all three cases is that, given the fact the bodies were moved after death, whoever killed them had to be strong and fit enough to do so. SOCO haven't found anything at the dump sites to suggest how that was accomplished."

Matt looked round at his team and silently thanked his lucky stars that he had such a coherent group to work with. He didn't envy Fabia with her problems with the LSCB committee.

"One last thing for all of you to concentrate on," Matt said. "I may be stating the obvious, but if you find any connection, however tenuous, that points towards a person or a group who would want all three of these men dead, report directly to me. There must be a link somewhere and we need to find it, as soon as possible. Thanks, everyone. Get back to work now."

# Chapter 18

"Sara and Chloe, can you give me a minute? I've got specific jobs for the two of you, and Aidan, can you get me the name of the woman who gave Geddings her phone number, please?"

"Okay, sir, coming right up." Aidan turned back to his desk and started tapping away at his keyboard.

The two women followed Matt into his office.

"First of all, Sara, I want you to find the recordings of those two anonymous tip-offs. Listen to them and see if anything stands out. You may be able to get some idea of who left them. Female, male, old, young, and whatever else occurs to you."

Sara nodded. "I'll do that now." She turned and went back to her desk.

"Chloe, for this you'll need to keep your family liaison training in mind since you'll probably be dealing with someone who's vulnerable. I want you to speak to the woman whose number Aidan is searching out. Give her a ring and see if you can persuade her to talk to us. It'd be best if it could be in person. If she's not happy with that, try to get her to give you as much information as you can over the phone."

At that moment, Aidan joined them. "That name you wanted, sir, it's Alys Penry and here's her phone number."

"Give them to Chloe, she'll take it from here."

"Sir" – Chloe sounded a little uneasy – "don't these scammers set up a completely false persona? How do you think I should approach this since the person that I'll be talking to will be describing a relationship with someone who amounts to a fictional character?"

"I see what you mean. Just bear that in mind when you speak to her. He might have slipped up and told her something that was real or true, and that could be useful to us."

"Okay, sir, I'll do my best."

Matt smiled at her. "You always do, Chloe."

"Thank you, sir."

She left his office with a spring in her step.

Once he was alone, Matt got out his mobile and dialled Fabia's number. When she picked up, he told her about the discovery of Huw Prosser's body and the similarities with the other two victims.

"We haven't been round to speak to Cath yet," he said, "but we're going to have to. She may have information that's useful to us. Maybe he told her things about his background that would help to find his killer."

"It's getting a bit spooky, isn't it?" said Fabia. "What on earth could these three men have in common? It's not as if they were known to each other."

"As far as we can tell."

"Granted. They were all guilty of criminal behaviour, but in totally different areas. I mean, what is there to connect a scammer, a drug dealer, and a stalker? It's really bugging me."

"Tell me about it," Matt said wearily. He looked up to see Dilys in his doorway. "Got to go, love, see you later."

Dilys came in as he ended the call. "The warrant to search that industrial unit has come through, sir. I suppose we should ask the Michaelsons for the keys."

"As a first step, send Tom and Craig, they'll be able to deal with any problems, then they can go on from there."

Some time later, Matt was going over some notes when a call came through from Tom.

"You got the keys okay, did you?"

"No problem. Paul and his mother said the place is nothing to do with them. It was Dai's business, not theirs, and insist they haven't been to check on it since before Dai was sent down."

"Have you been out to the warehouse?"

"Yes, sir. When we got there, it was obvious the place had been broken into. Whoever did so secured the door with a couple of cable ties. You'd better come and have a look at the place, sir, and get the SOCO team in. It's possible we might have found where at least one of the victims was killed. There seems to be a substantial amount of dried blood on the floor."

Matt didn't bother to ask for more details. "Okay, tell me the rest when I get there."

* * *

It took Matt and Dilys half an hour to get to the unit on an industrial site in Ringland. The whole place looked derelict. The road leading to the units was potholed, weeds and grass growing through cracks in the concrete path and around the edges of the metal-framed buildings. It didn't appear as if any of them were occupied. The roller doors on three of them were firmly closed, but the door had been pushed up on the unit furthest from the road. Tom's squad car was parked just outside. He and Craig got out and came to meet them.

"What have we got, Tom?" Matt asked.

"We haven't had a proper look, obviously, but there are definitely bloodstains on the floor; a lot in fact. There are a couple of office chairs, some rope littered about, and rolls of gaffer tape. That's what I've seen so far."

"Okay. I'll get through to Karen Johns – poor woman, she's being worked off her feet – and then we'll have a look. Can you get the kit out of the car, Dilys?"

Once they'd covered their shoes and put on gloves, leaving Craig to stand guard outside, the three of them made their way into the building, their footsteps echoing in the large empty space.

There were two shabby, black office chairs with wheels. One was on its side, the other upright. There was a rickety metal table and on it were two rolls of gaffer tape and a coil of rope. Under one of the chairs was another coil of rope. The bloodstains covered the floor by the overturned chair and there was blood on the chair itself.

"This definitely adds up when it comes to the first two victims," Dilys said.

"It certainly does," Matt agreed.

Matt and Dilys waited until the SOCO team arrived. As she climbed out of one of the vans, Karen was looking weary but determined.

"Bloody hell," she said, "this is beginning to get me down. I could do with a week off, preferably on a beach, in the sun, with plenty of chilled white wine on tap."

Matt smiled. "You and me both."

"I dare say you want my report yesterday?"

"Yup," Matt said, his smile widening. "I'll leave Craig and Tom to keep an eye on things. Dilys and I will get back to the station."

As they got into the car, Matt said, "On second thoughts, I think another word with the Michaelsons, mother and son, is in order. Let's pay them a visit on the way back."

"Good idea," said Dilys as she manoeuvred the car along the potholed road.

Their detour was useless. There was no answer when they rang the bell at the Michaelsons' flat and, once again, the next-door neighbour came out to speak to them.

"They're out," she told them. "Gone to see Dai in prison. Won't be back till late."

* * *

When they arrived at the office, both Sara and Chloe had news for Matt.

Sara had listened to the recordings of the anonymous calls relating to Seddon and brought her laptop in to let Matt have a listen. On both the recordings, the voice was obviously female, although it sounded muffled, as if an attempt had been made to disguise it. Matt listened to both messages, then listened to them again.

"Did you notice she says, 'I've watched him and read his notes'?" Matt said. "Surely that would mean the caller has to be someone who was close to him. On the second one, she says something like, 'He's gone out.' How did she know that if she isn't living in the same place, or nearby? It's possible these might have been left by his wife."

"I did wonder about that," Sara said.

"Can you make a hard copy of these two calls, Sara? I'd like to study them on the page."

"Will do, sir."

"Once I've read through them, I think another visit to Mrs Seddon could be useful."

Sara left his office looking pleased with herself.

"Okay, Chloe," Matt said, "what have you got for me?"

"I managed to get through to Alys Penry," she told him, "but she wouldn't talk to me over the phone. She did, however, give me her address. She lives in Knoll Road, the other side of Newport Golf Club. I got the impression she'd like to speak to us, to be reassured that he's alright, she said. I didn't tell her that he, well, wasn't. I think that's the sort of news to be given face to face."

"I agree."

"She did say she gets back from work – I'm not sure where she works – at four o'clock."

"Good. I suggest you and Dilys go and speak to her. What time is it? Half three. If you give it half an hour, then drive over there, hopefully she'll be home."

Chloe nodded but didn't leave his office. "There is another thing, like, an idea I've had."

Matt looked up and saw that her coffee-coloured cheeks had flushed a little. "And what was that?" he asked, smiling.

"I was thinking back to the idea that an investigative journalist might be involved. Like someone who's reported on the arrests and is angry the three men got away with their crimes."

"Go on."

"As you are aware, my brother Gareth is that sort of journalist. He's involved in a podcast called *Cold Case Cymru*, so he's used to doing research in this area. Do you think–"

The expression on Matt's face interrupted her.

"I'm not suggesting I should tell him anything I shouldn't," Chloe said quickly, "but thinking back to the Amber Morgan case, I remembered that Gareth searched out some useful information for us." She rushed on, her cheeks warming. "I could mention the bare bones of what we're investigating, some of which he'll know already because of newspaper reports and your press conference, and–"

Smiling, Matt held up a hand to stem the flow. "I think it'd be worth talking to him, but unofficially at the moment. You know the drill, and you can trust your brother, can't you? I don't want any of it getting on to his podcast."

"Absolutely not, sir," Chloe said earnestly.

"Go ahead, then, but take care of what you tell him," Matt said. "I look forward to hearing about anything he may turn up. Maybe you could speak to him after you and Dilys have visited Alys Penry and asked about Geddings."

* * *

Chloe parked the car outside the house not far from the golf club in Newport, turned to Dilys and asked, "How do you suggest we handle this?"

"Carefully," Dilys said.

They got out of the car and walked up to the front door. Dilys rang the bell and a few moments later it was opened by a small, pretty woman. The officers showed her their warrant cards.

"Oh," she said. "I was expecting you. Is there something wrong?"

"Sorry to disturb you, Ms Penry," Dilys said. "We're hoping you might be able to help us with a case we are working on. Would it be possible for us to come inside and have a chat?"

"Yes, of course. We'll go to the living room." Alys opened the door wider and showed the officers into a small, tidy room with a large window that provided a view of the golf course. "Please, take a seat. Would you like a cup of tea?"

"No, thank you," Dilys said, "but I'd like to record our conversation if you don't mind."

"Gosh that sounds serious but, no, I don't mind."

The group settled themselves as Dilys switched on her iPad, stated the date and who was present, then looked up at Alys.

"I'm afraid this is a little difficult," Dilys began. "We are investigating the murder of a man we believe you may have had some contact with online."

Alys covered her mouth with her hand. "Murder you say? Who are you talking about?"

"We have identified him as Seth Geddings, but you may well know him by a different name, Clint–"

"Oh my goodness! Yes, I do know him. You said he has been murdered? That's just awful."

"I'm sorry, but yes. His body was found on wasteland in Pontygwyn. Can you tell us how long ago you met him online?"

Alys dabbed at her eyes. "A while ago now, he seemed a nice man, very caring of his mother. She was sick, you see, needed urgent treatment and I was anxious to help."

"Did he ask you for money?" Chloe asked.

"Not directly, I think I offered some though. I don't like to think of anyone who can't obtain treatment." She smiled sadly. "We all know how the NHS is struggling."

"Did you actually give him any?" Dilys asked quietly.

"Well, no. We were about to finalise the loan when he dropped off the site. I've been worried about him, but not knowing where he lived, or having a phone number or anything for him, I didn't know how to look for him. I never thought he might have died."

"I know this is distressing for you and I'm afraid I have more bad news. The man was a scammer, fleecing money from many people online, men as well as women."

Alys gasped. "Oh no. That's dreadful, I thought… I…"

Chloe offered a tissue and the woman took it gratefully. "Can you tell us everything you know about him?" she asked. "We need to find out who killed him. We think the person responsible may have killed others."

"My good God!" said Alys. "This gets worse. I think I need a cuppa myself. This was not what I was expecting to hear today."

"I'll make us all some," Chloe said and got to her feet. "You stay here and talk to Dilys. Anything you can tell us will be useful."

* * *

That evening, Matt found Fabia in the kitchen feeding Bethan, who spotted her da and waved sticky, chubby fingers at him.

"How are my girls?" he asked, kissing Fabia on the cheek, and ruffling his daughter's hair.

"We're good," Fabia said. "We've been waiting for you. Have you had another busy day?"

"They all are at the moment and nothing is going to change in the near future." He dragged a hand down his face. "I'd be happier if we were making more progress, and I've got a pile of interviews lined up for tomorrow."

"Who will you be talking to?" Fabia asked as she poured two glasses of whisky and placed one in front of Matt on the table.

"Cath is first on the list."

"I'm not sure how useful she'll be." Fabia sat at the table. "I spoke to her earlier and she told me Huw didn't talk much about his past. She's still very distressed about what happened. Her face is badly bruised and now she is wondering whether she should take the services this week, afraid she'll frighten her parishioners. I can't believe what has happened. I hope you'll be gentle with her tomorrow."

"Why wouldn't I be?" Matt asked. "She's a victim after all."

"Maybe I should be there?"

"There's really no need. Don't you trust me?"

Fabia patted Matt's hand. "Of course I do but she is very fragile and I don't think the rural dean is being particularly helpful. I've advised her to take some time off, go away for a couple of days until she feels better. What makes a man like Prosser do such awful things?"

"If I knew the answer to that, I could retire. I keep thinking about Sky Laska, the woman who killed herself. I think the vicar has had a lucky escape."

"Yes, I agree. Have you managed to track down the black cab Prosser's neighbour reported seeing?"

Matt rubbed his eyes. "No. It's a dead end. No London cab is on any of the local taxi firm's books, and the DVLA have said there isn't one registered locally. It is possible she was mistaken. Consequently we haven't been able to discover who was with the victim the night he was taken from the house, and the description from the neighbour was pretty vague."

"What else will you be doing tomorrow?" Fabia asked as she lifted Bethan from her high chair and handed her to Matt for a *cwtch*.

"After speaking to Cath, Dilys and I are planning to have another word with the Michaelsons, ask them about what was found in the warehouse. I can't believe they don't know anything about it."

"They might not. I don't think Paul was involved with all of Dai's operations, and if it was Dai's place and they told you they'd never been there, maybe they haven't."

"I know, but how much of what they told us was the truth?"

Matt got his feet and swung his daughter into the air. "Come on, my lovely, let's get you bathed and ready for bed, then me and your mam will eat supper and have an early night. I'm utterly shattered."

# Chapter 19

Chloe Daniels and her brother, Gareth, had a favourite pub, the Red Dragon, just along the road from the flat that Gareth shared with his partner, Theresa. That evening, when Chloe arrived, Gareth was already standing at the bar talking to the barman.

He greeted Chloe with a smile.

"Did Theresa mind not coming?" she asked him.

"Not at all, it's her Pilates evening. She said to remind you that you're having lunch at ours on Sunday. Now, what'll you have?"

"A large glass of red, preferably a Shiraz. It's been mad at work and I need a pick-me-up."

They took their drinks to a table in a quiet corner and sat down.

"So, what's all this about?" Gareth asked.

"It's a bit awkward, in a way. The chief said I could talk to you in an unofficial capacity. I got the impression he won't mind if I stretch the rules a bit, but you're not to put any of it into your podcast, understood?"

"Of course not," said Gareth, the picture of innocence. "Would I ever do a thing like that?"

"I mean it, Gareth. This is serious stuff."

His grin faded. "Okay. Agreed. What's up?"

Chloe took a gulp of her wine then looked around the pub. A few customers were seated at small tables around the dimly lit room, but most of the punters were over by the bar. In spite of this, she leant towards her brother and lowered her voice. "You've probably seen press coverage of the cases we're dealing with at the moment."

"I saw your boss conducting a press conference. Something to do with a body found on wasteland in Pontygwyn. Is that one of them?"

"Yes," Chloe said, "and there are two other murders connected to it."

"We've reported them, but I've not been assigned to the stories. Where were the other two found, and what's the connection?"

Chloe described the murders and filled in the details on each victim.

"I'm convinced there's some kind of revenge motive involved," she told him, "which would mean we need to find someone who knew all three victims. So far, we've failed. Each of the victims had been arrested in the past but never prosecuted. I suggested to the boss that an investigative journalist might be involved. Someone who's become obsessed with criminals who have gotten away with it and decided to take matters into their own hands.

Gareth took a swig of his pint. "It wouldn't be hard to find out about unsuccessful convictions. There's plenty of information out there."

"Yes, and there might be a connection to a nasty piece of work called Dai Michaelson–"

"The Michaelson gang?" Gareth interrupted her. "I've heard of them alright. A pair of brothers to be avoided at all costs, quite apart from any of the associates they may have. If your victims were involved with them, it would be easy to dig into their track record."

Chloe told her brother about the broken fingers and the cuts. "The problem, for the killer, is that Dai is holed up in jail, which is a pretty good alibi. Dilys, Sergeant Bevan, thinks that the younger Michaelson, Paul, may be copying his brother's shitty habits, but I'm not sure about that. I haven't had direct contact with either of them. So that's what made me think we could be dealing with someone who knows their tactics."

"I can do some digging for you." He took a gulp of his pint, then his eyes widened. "Now I come to think of it, there is someone that might fit the bill for your obsessed journalist, although whether he'd go so far as to kill someone is another matter."

"Tell me," Chloe said, leaning forward.

"He's a bloke who's been hanging round the office for a few weeks, he's a pain actually, and a bit of a weirdo. I'd say he's around fiftyish, a big, lumbering bloke. His name's Keith Prendergast. The editor told us he's writing a book on local newspaper coverage through the years and asked us to give him as much help as possible. I think they're probably old buddies from way back."

"Is he local?" Chloe asked.

"I'm pretty sure he comes from round here, but I can double-check."

"You said he's a bit of a weirdo, in what way?" Chloe asked.

Gareth screwed up his face. "He sort of creeps around. One minute he's at the desk he's been given to work at, the next you look round and he's just behind you, sort of looming, and he has this very soft voice, high-pitched, which doesn't match his size at all."

"I don't suppose he can help his voice."

"I suppose not," Gareth said.

"Has he shown any interest in the murders we're dealing with?"

"Yes, come to think of it, he has." Gareth pushed his pint glass towards Chloe and grinned. "Your round, then I'll tell you the rest."

Chloe made a face at her brother then battled her way to the bar and back. She plonked Gareth's pint in front of him. "Okay. Stop teasing. Out with it!"

"It was a couple of days ago. I was in the canteen and he sidled up and asked if he could join me, then proceeded to give me the third degree about your job."

"Gareth!" Chloe protested. "Why didn't you tell me?"

"I was going to."

"How did he find out I'm in the police?"

"He said he'd heard me talking to Vanessa – you know, one of our receptionists – well, boasting, I suppose, about you adding family liaison to your qualifications."

"That was a year ago," Chloe said. "I'm back in the chief inspector's team now."

"I know, but she'd asked about what it entailed. She's thinking of applying to join the force with the specific intention of doing something in that area. Anyway, he had been earwigging our conversation and, when I got back upstairs, that's when he came and asked me again about your job."

"I sincerely hope you didn't tell him anything."

Gareth smiled. "As little as possible. He took the hint and pushed off."

"Good. So tell me, are you up for having a bit of a dig around about the murders?"

"Of course, sis, anything for you."

"Good to know, but for goodness sake, be discreet. I don't want to get into trouble with the chief inspector."

# Chapter 20

The next morning, Matt and Dilys drove to the vicarage to talk with Cath Temple. The weather was kind and the traffic from Newport light.

"It's a shame Alys Penry didn't know anything that would help us with Geddings," Matt said.

"Yes, she was very upset when we told her. I find it really sad how some folk are drawn into these romance scams. They're lonely, I guess. But when we do catch anyone who's at it, they nearly all walk away. I don't think the government takes this sort of crime anywhere near seriously enough, yet so much damage is done. The victims always feel ashamed, which is why so many people don't come forward to report these crimes."

"I couldn't agree more, but every time we nick one, ten more pop up. Not long ago, fraudsters needed to face you, not hide behind false identities and never leave their rooms. They are difficult crimes to solve."

"The internet makes everything easier," Dilys said, "crimes as well as banking and other legitimate uses. Regulation needs to be tightened."

"Again I agree, but we'd need to double the police force if that happened. Most coppers don't understand the way the internet works, which is why I'm grateful for Aidan."

Dilys pulled up outside the vicarage, turned off the engine and together they walked up the path and rang the bell. A few moments passed before it was opened and Cath Temple peered out. Matt winced when he saw the bruising on her face and understood why she might not be keen to preach on Sunday.

"Hallo, both of you," Cath said. "Come to the kitchen and I'll put the kettle on." The stout woman set off along the hall followed by the detectives. "Please, take a seat."

"Gosh, Cath," Matt said as they settled themselves at the table, "Fabia told me your face was bruised, but I didn't expect it to look so bad. Are you okay? Have you seen a doctor?"

"There's no need for that," Cath said as she poured boiling water into a teapot and carried it to the table. "I've decided to take a long weekend off. The rural dean will arrange a replacement to take the Sunday services."

"I think that's a good idea," Dilys said. "Is there anything we can do you help you?"

"That's kind, but I don't think so, thank you." Cath frowned. "I know it isn't a very nice thing to say, but at least I know he won't bother me again. Any idea who might have killed him?"

"No," Matt said, "and the main reason we are here is to talk about his last visit."

"Yes, I thought it might be."

Dilys removed her tablet and switched it on. "You have no objection to me recording our conversation, do you?"

"None at all."

Dilys smiled, stated who was in the room and the date, then smiled at Cath. "Rightio then, let's make a start. Can you tell us exactly what happened when Huw Prosser attacked you?"

Cath took a deep breath and recounted what had happened. Matt and Dilys listened carefully, without interrupting, until she reached the end of her story.

"Thank you," Matt said, "that was very clear. I am very sorry that happened to you."

Cath offered a weak smile. "It was hardly your fault, Matt."

"Maybe not, but I should have been firmer when I kicked him out the other evening. I honestly didn't think he would do something like this."

Cath waved away his comment and topped up the mugs. "Now you've heard my sorry tale, is there something I can do for you?"

"Possibly. Obviously we are now investigating the murder of your stalker and don't know much about his background," Matt said. "During your–" he paused "–association with the man, did he tell you anything about his life that might be useful?"

"Probably not," Cath admitted, "he didn't talk much about himself or his life, just that he had moved to the area, was a committed Christian, and wanted to become involved at St Cybi's. As you know, he was a sidesman and a regular worshipper."

"So the other worshippers liked him?"

"I'm not sure I'd go as far as that."

"Why do you say that?"

"He was always pushy, tried to get too involved with other members of the congregation. Single women in the main." Cath rubbed her eyes. "I should have picked up on it, done something, but…"

"Situations like this are difficult," Matt said, "but you shouldn't blame yourself. This is *his* fault – not yours."

"Thank you for saying so, Matt. I have always been grateful for the friendship you and Fabia have shown me."

Matt smiled. "Don't be daft, we're both very fond of you too. You said you're taking some time off. Are you planning a proper break for a few days?"

"I thought I would, so I am going to visit my sister. Could you let Fabia know I'll be away? I should be back in the middle of next week."

"Of course, and if you need anything in the meantime, just give one of us a ring." He got to his feet as Dilys switched off her tablet and tucked it away. "I'm sorry, we have to get off now, but don't forget – you know where we are."

Cath nodded and saw them out. They went to the car and Dilys started the engine.

"Poor Cath," she said. "I hate cases like this, when good people fall foul of bad people. The laws on stalking are too lax."

"I agree. Such a shame she couldn't tell us anything we didn't already know." Matt dragged a hand down his face. "Okay then, let's get on. We'll leave the Michaelsons until later in the day, I want to have a word with Mrs Seddon now. I hope we will be able to make some progress soon. By the end of the day, I must have something to tell the chief super. I know the press are giving her a hard time and don't want her to give me one."

"Rightio, sir."

* * *

Twenty-five miles and fifty minutes later, Dilys pulled up outside the Seddon residence.

"I wonder how things were before the strikes in the eighties when the pits were still open and there were plenty of jobs," she said.

"You probably wouldn't recognise these streets," Matt said. "Kids out playing, their mams scrubbing doorsteps and windows to keep the coal dust from building up, gossips chatting over the back fences, and gangs of miners marching home, boots clattering on the cobbles."

"Gosh, sir, it sounds as though you were there, but I know you're not old enough."

"Plenty of old photos around now, heaps online and you know how I like local history." He opened the passenger door. "Come on, then. Let's see what Gwyneth Seddon has to say. I know she's withholding information. How is it possible she did not know what her creative chemist husband was up to?"

"Not impossible, sir. Husbands and wives often keep stuff from each other, especially if they know their partner wouldn't approve."

"I suppose, but I'm not convinced, and we need to push harder." He smiled at her. "I am experiencing what Fabia might call 'a hunch'."

Dilys laughed. "Are you? I can't wait to tell her what you've just said."

"We could keep it between ourselves."

Dilys shook her head and was still giggling as Matt hammered on the door of the Seddons' house. He knocked a second time and eventually the door opened and Gwyneth Seddon peered out.

"Oh," she said, "it's you again. Haven't you bothered me enough? I've already told you everything I know and just want to be left in peace."

"We're sorry to disturb you, madam," Dilys said, "but we are still investigating your husband's death." She lowered her voice. "You may have heard but another man has been murdered and we must catch whoever's doing this. It is possible they may kill again."

Gwyneth's hand flew to her mouth and her eyes widened.

Dilys continued, "You can see how important this is and it would be much better to talk inside, if you wouldn't mind."

"Is it true? Someone else has died?" The woman glanced at Matt, who nodded. "You had better come in then," she said and held open the door.

She directed them to the front room where they sat on the sofa. She took a nearby easy chair and clasped her hands together tightly in her lap. "Can you tell me who was killed?"

"His name was Huw Prosser," Matt said. "He lived in Newport. Do you know the name?"

Gwyneth shook her head. "No, not that I recall, although it is a common name."

"He was also known as Harry Pierce. Did your husband ever mention the man?"

"No, but he didn't mention much. As I've told you, he was a private man and, as long as he brought in a wage, I didn't pry."

Dilys leaned forward in her seat. "Hardly prying, Mrs Seddon, taking an interest in your husband's job."

The woman didn't answer, merely turned her gaze to the front window and stared out at the quiet street.

Dilys tried again. "I'm very sorry, madam, and I know how hard this is for you, but it is very important."

"As you know," Matt said, "your husband had been interviewed on a couple of occasions in relation to the manufacture and distribution of both illegal and counterfeit drugs." He sucked in a deep breath. "We are not accusing you of being involved in his schemes, but if you know anything, anything at all, please help us."

"The police have received anonymous tip-offs in the past which is why your husband was investigated. Is it possible you might know something about those calls?" Dilys said.

Gwyneth covered her face in her hands and her shoulders shook as she began sobbing. Matt and Dilys kept quiet and exchanged glances. Gwyneth pulled a tissue from her sleeve, dried her face and blew her nose. She looked up at Dilys with red eyes.

"It was me," she said voice barely above a whisper. "I made the calls."

"You did?" Dilys asked gently, trying not to sound surprised. "Can you tell me why?"

The distressed woman gulped and dabbed frantically at her overflowing eyes. "Because I didn't want him here, didn't want to live with him any longer. I thought you would come and arrest him, like you did last time. Only last time you didn't send him to prison, you sent him home to me and I couldn't bear it."

"Was he violent to you?' Dilys asked.

"Not in the way you think." Gwyneth took a breath. "I hated him for making those filthy drugs, but he wouldn't stop even though I begged him to. All that happened was he yelled at me and told me I had to keep quiet." Her voice dropped even lower and Dilys leaned closer to catch her words. "Then–" she swallowed hard "–then those beautiful girls died, the twins, and I knew… I bloody knew he was to blame. People were so angry. What would happen if everyone found out? What would they think of me? I wouldn't have been safe and it wasn't like I could have stopped him."

No, Matt thought, you couldn't, but you could have made a proper statement at the time. By not speaking out you perverted the course of justice, and others might have been poisoned.

"Anyway," Gwyneth continued, "we rowed even worse, horrid it was. Eventually he left. I didn't know where he went and didn't care. I didn't even tell anyone he had left; all I knew was that I could breathe again. Until now, that is."

Dilys passed over a handful of tissues and patted the older woman's arm. "Well done, madam."

Matt did feel some sympathy for her, but had to work hard at keeping a smile off his face in appreciation of his sergeant's skill. The way Dilys encouraged the reluctant and unwilling to talk was nothing short of a superpower.

"You know," Gwyneth said, "after what my husband did, I'm glad he's dead. He deserved nothing less, and the world is a better place."

* * *

As time was getting on when they left, Matt made the decision to head back to the station and brief the team with the new information. Dilys drove and they travelled in silence, contemplating what they had learned. The weather had remained good and Matt gazed out the side window at the passing countryside, smiling when he spotted gangs of tiny lambs charging around on the new spring grass, their mothers keeping a watchful eye from a distance.

Arriving in Newport nearly an hour later, Dilys dropped her boss at the back door and went to park the car. Matt walked upstairs to his office and had barely settled behind his desk when Chloe tapped on his door and walked in.

"How did you get on, sir?" she asked.

"Fair to middling. Mrs Seddon was willing to talk – at last – but we didn't make it to the Michaelsons, that will have to wait until Monday."

"I've put the team on notice that you will brief them this afternoon, and Karen Johns was here earlier looking for you."

Matt raised his eyebrows. "Did she say what she wanted?"

"No, sir."

"Okay. I'll give her a ring while I grab a coffee and wait for Dilys. Did you have any luck tracing that black cab?"

"No, sir. Definitely none registered locally, either privately or at one of the local firms. It's almost as though it never existed."

"So, little chance of tracking down whoever escorted Huw Prosser from his house then." Matt sighed. "Okay, give me a minute or two to make a couple of calls and I'll be right there."

Chloe nodded and left the office. Matt fetched himself a coffee, then sat behind his desk and, after providing Dilys with a brief update, dialled Karen Johns' number. He was pleased when she answered almost immediately.

"Thank you for getting back to me, sir," she said.

"I'm sorry it wasn't sooner, but Dilys and I got caught up with the second victim's wife. To be honest, I'm not entirely sure it takes us anywhere, but at least we've managed to tie up another loose end."

"That is always satisfying, and I might be able to tie up another for you."

Matt sat up straighter. "Oh?"

"I went back out to all three body dumps today. I often need to take some time so I can return to a scene with fresh eyes, and it often works. You know how it is – stare at something long enough and you miss stuff."

"Were your visits productive?" Matt asked, feeling his heart beat faster.

He could hear the smile on her face. "They were." She paused and took a breath. "I'm pretty sure I know how the bodies were moved. That was bugging me more than I can say. I just couldn't work out how they could have been moved without a vehicle and there was no sign of that."

Matt chuckled softly. "Don't tell me, you plumped for horsepower?"

"No, but my fresh eyes have borne fruit." Karen then told him in great detail what she had found at all three sites.

"That certainly sounds plausible," Matt said. "Jolly well done."

"I have documented the areas and further tests will be undertaken so there is no doubt, but for now I have some photographs I could e-mail over."

"That would be great, thanks. I'm about to brief the team and this will give them more to work on."

"I'll send them now."

Matt put the phone down and smiled when an e-mail pinged in a minute or two later. The smile grew as he opened the attachments and sent them to the printer. He waited as the sheets spilled out then gathered them together, slipped on his jacket and made his way to the main office with a spring in his step.

“Look lively, everyone,” he said and waved the small bundle in the air. “It seems as though SOCO has come up trumps and given us some new evidence to work with.”

# Chapter 21

Matt arrived home late and found Fabia sitting at the table, her laptop open in front of her. He moved closer and kissed her cheek before sitting opposite her.

"I'm sorry I'm so late," he said. "I've missed Bethan's bath time again." He smiled weakly. "Have I also missed supper?"

"I guessed you might be late so I didn't cook, but I can round up some cold meat, and cheese and pickle with crusty bread. Is that any use to you?"

"Sounds perfect, thank you. Can I help?"

"No, stay where you are and tell me about your day."

Matt did as she asked and by the time his meal appeared on the table he had told Fabia about his visit to Cath and the enlightening chat with Gwyneth Seddon.

"Is it possible she killed her husband?" Fabia asked as she poured two glasses of wine. "It certainly sounds as though she was very angry with him."

"Oh she was certainly that, alright, but I can't see her as a killer. I don't believe she has any fight left in her at all, it seems Seddon was a bully and wore her down. Anyway, what reason would she have for killing Geddings and Prosser?"

"I don't know. Perhaps she had been hooked into one of Geddings' scams."

"Okay, for argument's sake, let's say she was taken in. Are you suggesting she was also stalked by Prosser? That's too much of a coincidence for my liking. I work on facts, hard facts."

"Yes, I know you do. So what did Karen Johns tell you?"

"If I can borrow your laptop, I'll show you. I'd welcome your opinion."

Fabia smiled, secretly pleased he was willing to share evidence with her and twisted the device towards him. He logged onto his e-mail account, tapped for a couple of minutes more, then swivelled the laptop back towards her.

She peered at the screen. "What am I looking at?" she asked.

"Photographs taken at all three sites of impressions discovered in the mud – tyre tracks, to be exact." Matt leaned back in his chair looking pleased with himself.

Fabia peered closer. "What were they left by? Kids on bikes perhaps?"

"Too narrow to be bikes, too light a tread – or so Karen tells me."

"So what then? A pram, child's buggy – something like that? Go-kart maybe? How would anyone move a full-size body in a pram?"

"Karen says the marks were left by a wheelchair."

Fabia took a moment to allow the new information to sink in. "Oh my goodness," she said eventually. "What an inventive way of moving a body without drawing attention to yourself."

"Exactly! Let's be honest here, who pays much notice of someone being pushed in a wheelchair? Bundle them up in blankets and no one would take a second glance."

Fabia laughed. "Such a great piece of work by SOCO. Can Karen narrow down the model of the chair?"

"She's going to give it a go, but doesn't hold out much hope. The tyres used on chairs are all pretty similar, unless you're talking about a racing chair or a cross-country version – specialist rather than standard issue."

"Are you going to release this? Make an appeal for any witnesses to come forward to report possible sightings?"

"I don't know. I'll be speaking to Erica Talbot first thing Monday morning and it's her call to make."

Fabia frowned. "Another early start then?"

"Yes, sorry, my love, but I want to keep moving forward now the case is making progress."

"I understand, I'd want to do the same." She reached across the table and took his hand. "You're looking tired, *cariad*. I worry about you."

Matt was surprised, he expected to be nagged about not spending enough time with Bethan. "Thank you," he said, "but you don't need to worry. You know what it is like to work such a large investigation." He raised her hand to his mouth and brushed a kiss on the back of it. "I feel good about this though. Now I reckon we have a chance of catching the killer." He let go her hand and got to his feet. "I'll just go and check on our little chick, then I need a shower."

"Just make sure you don't disturb her. She's still having trouble with her teeth and it took me a long time to get her off."

* * *

On Monday morning, after Matt had left for work, Fabia gave Bethan her breakfast, then settled her in the playpen with a favourite teddy and a teething ring. Once she was certain her daughter was content, she cleared the kitchen table and covered it with sheets of paper, coloured pens, and the notes she had made relating to the cases Matt was working on. Before she began to construct a mind map, she read through everything she knew about the murders, the victims and the people around them.

When everything was fresh in her mind, she took three different coloured pens and wrote the names of the victims in a line across the centre of a large sheet of white paper. Around each name she added more names – relatives, friends of the deceased, others who'd had contact with them; some close, some less so.

She got to her feet, leaned into the playpen to ruffle Bethan's coppery curls, then made a fresh coffee. She carried the mug back to the table and stared at the result of her labours: a colourful design of lines, circles and scribbled notes. She sat and focused on the names of the victims in the centre and tried to bring them into her mind. She thought about Prosser first, remembered the nickname Geraldine had given him, and smiled. She remembered him as the unpleasant Harry Pierce. He had a smarmy air and was full of himself, puffing up at every available opportunity like a rooster on heat. He had form too. Maybe he had left other victims in his wake who might have wanted to settle a score. Fabia took a red pen and wrote 'Harry Pierce' beneath Huw Prosser, together with a note – 'more research'.

Next, she turned her attention to Jake Seddon, the first victim and someone she had also met during the investigation into his drug-making activities a few years ago. She remembered how angry Gwyn Jones had still been with the man when she'd visited him with Bethan. He was certainly convinced that the death of the twins in Newport could be dropped firmly on Seddon's doorstep. Could he be angry enough to kill? Fabia shook her head. Gwyn had been a decent copper, a good one too, who hated injustice like all coppers, but he'd never break the law in such a drastic manner. She recalled interviewing Seddon; how cocky and self-important he had been. How he threw accusations of wrongful arrest around like autumn leaves; threatened them with 'the best solicitors'. His wife didn't like him either. In fact, she had detested him from what Matt had said. Was she a killer? Matt said that she didn't have it in her, but

Fabia knew everyone had it in them given the correct trigger. She underlined Gwyneth Seddon and turned her attention to the last victim.

She didn't know so much about Seth Geddings and, as far as she knew, had never met him. Another criminal up to no good who had managed to keep one step ahead of the law and never faced charges. She wasn't surprised. Cases like his were beyond most ordinary coppers and needed someone like Aidan to unpick them. Even then, the CPS had to be convinced of something they didn't really understand either. The evidence was more ethereal. No blood, or DNA, or footprints in the mud, or CCTV, but keystrokes and code twisted in a certain way. She did know, though, how much distress and pain and chaos someone like that could cause to others online; those who were lonely and searching for something. Fabia felt anger rise in her own chest and tried to imagine how she would feel if she'd lost her life savings, having been taken in by a man professing undying love. What would she be capable of under such circumstances?

Bethan suddenly rolled over a little enthusiastically, banged her head on the edge of the playpen and began squawking loudly. Fabia shot to her feet, lifted her daughter into her arms and held her close to her chest, rocking and cooing. Within a few minutes, Bethan was smiling again and Fabia knew how blessed she was to have such a happy child.

* * *

"Well," Erica Talbot said as she leaned back in her chair at the end of Matt's briefing, "at last, progress is being made." Matt opened his mouth to defend his team, but Erica held up her hand. "I'm not being critical, Inspector, merely speaking the truth. This is a multi-layered murder investigation and, while I might pray for a quick resolution, I know that in reality something this complex will not be solved overnight."

Matt nodded. "Thank you, ma'am. What is your view about making the public aware of the possible involvement of a wheelchair?"

"I'm torn about that. It's such a distinctive way of getting rid of a body that I don't really want the killer to know that we know. It would be short work to dump any chair in the river never to be seen again, and we'd potentially lose crucial evidence." She paused and thought a moment. "No, we should keep this close to our chests, but make sure the team know about it, just in case they manage to arrest a suspect" – she smiled – "and find he has a wheelchair in the shed."

"I agree," Matt said. "Karen Johns is still working with the tyre impressions collected at the three sites and has confirmed a definite match, something to do with a scuffed or worn patch on one of the tyres. She says if we find the chair that matches what she has, we can prove it was at the body dumps."

Erica nodded. "We have some good evidence, much more than we're lucky to recover in many other cases, yet we still haven't put it together. You would think the wounds on the victims' chests and their broken fingers would lead us straight to a suspect – and it does – but Dai Michaelson, as we know, is in custody. Are you absolutely sure his brother hasn't had anything to do with this?"

Matt shrugged. "To be honest, I can't be sure." Matt paused then said, "As you suspect, I have discussed the case with Fabia."

Erica smiled. "I would be very surprised and disappointed if you hadn't. Your partner has a first-rate mind and is wasted as chair of the LSCB. If I had my way, she'd be back where she belongs, as a member of the team."

Matt felt himself glow with pride and tried not to grin like the proverbial cat that got the cream.

"Has she made any suggestions about the direction she thinks the investigation should go?" Erica asked.

"Not yet, but she has promised me one of her mind maps. They've always proved useful in the past – even if I don't fully understand how she creates them."

"Okay, good. Are you closer to tracking down any family Prosser might have?"

"Unfortunately not. His home has been searched, but we found nothing there to suggest he has any. Chloe is trying to dig into his background, but with him using two names it has been more difficult than it should." Matt dragged a hand over his face. "It's as though he suddenly appeared as Pierce, then reinvented himself here as Prosser. Even though he was questioned in connection with the suicide of Sky Laska, he wasn't arrested so there's no DNA on record. We'll keep at it."

"Yes, do that." She got to her feet. "What have you on the cards for today?"

"Dilys and I have planned a second chat with Cari and Paul Michaelson, and I'm going to take another walk around their warehouse. I want to make sure nothing has been missed. The discovery of a possible mini lab on site provides a tentative link to our renegade chemist, Jake Seddon. The others must be linked too, but so far what the link is has eluded us, I'm afraid."

Erica nodded and opened the door. "Make sure to keep me informed, Matt, and please pass on my regards to Fabia and Bethan."

"I will."

Matt walked downstairs and found Dilys waiting for him in his office. She looked up from her laptop as he entered.

"How was it, sir?" she asked.

"About what you'd expect. Right then, let's make tracks. Michaelsons first, then another visit to the warehouse."

# Chapter 22

The spring sunshine of the day before had been blotted out by a thick layer of grey clouds. A stiff wind swirled around Matt and Dilys as they left the car and walked up to the front door of the Michaelsons'. Dilys knocked loudly on the door and it was opened a couple of minutes later by Cari. It appeared she had just got out of bed; her face was creased from the pillow and she was dressed in pink pyjamas with kittens printed on the material.

"Christ, not you lot again," she grouched. "Haven't you got anything better to do than keep on bothering us? I've barely opened my bloody eyes."

"I'm sorry, madam," Dilys said, "but we are conducting a murder investigation. As we work the case, more questions are bound to present themselves. Is your son here?"

"He's in bed. You'd better come in."

Cari turned away from the door and headed towards the kitchen. She put the kettle on, removed a cigarette from a packet on the table, lit it and then coughed loudly as her lungs protested. Matt winced and perched on a stool next to the counter. Dilys removed her tablet and prepared to record the conversation. Cari frowned but didn't pass comment.

"Get on with it then," she said, "I have stuff to do today."

Matt thought that was unlikely. "Could you wake your son? We'd like to speak to him too."

Cari frowned, but shuffled out of the kitchen and returned a few minutes later with Paul, who was dressed in T-shirt, boxers and woolly socks. He plonked himself on a chair and glared at the officers.

"I don't get why you're here again," he said. "We've told you more than once we don't know anything, so you should be out there catching the bad guy, not bothering us."

"In any investigation new questions come up and we must ask them or we wouldn't be doing our jobs properly," Matt said.

"So ask, then be on your way."

"We have reason to believe that your cousin-in-law, Jake Seddon, was using the warehouse Dai owns for producing illegal and counterfeit drugs. Evidence was found of a temporary laboratory set up in the back of the place. Do either of you know anything about that?"

"We've already told you we don't," Cari snapped. "We didn't get involved with anything that went on in the warehouse, that was down to Dai. You should ask him."

"Yes, we will, but you may have heard there has been another murder. Paul, where were you on Thursday evening and night from about five o'clock?"

Paul seemed to consider this. He looked at his mother. "I was here wasn't I, Mam?" he said.

Cari puffed aggressively on her cigarette. "Of course you were, Paul love. We were in all night."

Dilys removed an enlarged photograph of Huw Prosser from her bag and placed it on the table. "Do you know this man?" she asked.

Cari barely glanced at the image and shook her head. "Never seen him before."

"Could you take a proper look, please?" Dilys asked. "It is very important. How about you, Paul, do you recognise him?"

"No. Like Mam, I've never seen him before."

"He was found on the banks of the river Usk. He had been mistreated before his death and like the other victims, his fingers had been broken. That was your brother's calling card, wasn't it? When he was running the protection racket, those who couldn't or wouldn't pay, had their fingers snapped."

"So you say," Paul sneered. "I still say he was set up. It's what the police do, stitch people up to keep the crime numbers down."

"That isn't true," Matt said. "There was video footage of your brother's vicious attack on the shopkeeper. It was an open-and-shut case and he was found unanimously guilty by the jury at his trial. He hasn't even behaved himself in prison and is now serving a second sentence." He took a deep breath. "It is difficult for us to believe that you haven't continued with the family business."

"I don't care what you believe," Cari said. "You can't prove my boy has done anything and until you can, you should sling your hook. This is harassment and there are laws about that. I've told you, Paul had nothing to with any of this, and you haven't found any evidence to say that he has." She snorted. "You even took him down the station and had to let him go. It's not right, it isn't, so unless you intend to arrest him you must leave. Right now!"

"Okay," Matt said, "have it your way, but you need to be aware that we will more than likely be back."

"And you need to be aware that unless you bring a warrant, you won't be getting in."

Matt got to his feet. Dilys turned off the tablet, tucked it away and they walked out to the car.

"That didn't go well, sir," Dilys said.

"Not especially, no, and she's right of course. We don't have enough to arrest her son." Matt groaned.

"Let's get over to the warehouse. Maybe we'll have more luck there."

* * *

Ten minutes later, Dilys pulled up on the access road outside the row of warehouses. Matt got out of the car, shivered, and turned up the collar of his coat. A bitter wind, chilled by its passage over the Black Mountains, barrelled along the narrow corridor between the buildings and a high, brick wall. Dilys left the car and pulled her coat tighter.

"I've lived in Wales all my life," she said, "but the sudden weather shifts still catch me out. It was beautiful yesterday."

"It'll be Easter soon," Matt said. "Did you know the UK is much more likely to have a white Easter than a white Christmas?" He looked up at the dark sky then walked towards the door of the warehouse. He unlocked a shiny new padlock, tore away a remnant of blue and white police tape and opened the door.

The large, cavernous space was dimly lit. Matt found a light switch but when he tried it, nothing happened. They waited a while for their eyes to adjust to the gloom. Dilys switched on the light on her mobile phone and illuminated a myriad of gently swirling dust motes.

"Where exactly was the suspected laboratory found?" Matt asked.

"Rear left-hand corner. Not much was found though; some small scraps of paper were recovered, with chemical names printed on them, some battered equipment, trays and broken scales. It was decided there had been some sort of manufacturing going on, but it was a loose end. As you know, Jake Seddon was questioned, but there wasn't enough to charge him, and with his solicitor breathing fire down our necks, he was released. Proper chopsy that solicitor is, I've come across him since."

"Anything further come in regarding the blood that was found here?"

"I'm afraid not, sir."

Matt snorted loudly. "Okay then," he said. "Let's take a slow wander around the place and keep our eyes open. I'm sure there must be something we missed before."

"Have you got another hunch, sir?"

Matt frowned at her, so she stifled a giggle and fell in by his side. The place was pretty much empty. The chair, table and other evidence found had been recovered and all that remained was the odd smear of blood. Matt's stomach twisted as he tried to imagine what had taken place there. The immediate area had been swept clean, the dust and debris collected for examination by the forensic labs, but nothing else of use had been discovered. He began a second lap of the building and walked slowly along the back wall.

"Sir," Dilys said, "I think I've found something."

Matt retraced his steps. "Show me," he said.

Dilys pointed low down at the wall. "See that cable by there? That's an internet connection, that is."

"So what? A place like this would probably need it. Wi-Fi is rubbish around here."

"That cable is new, recently installed. No way is it five years old and that's how long Dai Michaelson has been locked up. His mam and brother maintain they have never been here, so who has? Maybe it was our scammer – Seth Geddings."

"I think that's a leap. We found his kit in the room above the Chinese takeaway."

"Well, we're not making much progress so we need to consider different scenarios. If Geddings had been using this place and the Michaelsons found out about it, I'm sure they wouldn't be delighted. Or they knew; rented him some space perhaps and he didn't pay what he owed them. They might even have distributed Seddon's wares. We need to find the link, sir, and it stands to reason that the victims must all have known their killer – or killers. If the premise is that Seddon cooked his drugs here, why not consider that Geddings committed his crimes here too?"

Matt dragged a hand down his face. "Okay, I'll bear it in mind, but we need hard evidence, not scenarios." He turned away from the wall and suddenly stopped walking. He removed his phone from his pocket and was pleased to see that not only did he have a signal, but some battery life too. He tapped in a number and waited for his call to be answered.

"Chief Inspector," a woman's voice said. "Can I help you with something?"

"I hope so, Karen. Dilys and I are at the warehouse owned by Dai Michaelson and think we might have found something. Have you got time to pop over with those fresh eyes of yours and take a look?"

"As it happens, I have an hour or so. Stay where you are, and I'll meet you there."

* * *

When Matt and Dilys made it back to the office, they found Aidan perched on one of the desks chatting to Chloe. They looked up as they entered.

"Sir," Aidan called. "Have you got a moment or two to spare?"

"Certainly, if you have something useful to tell me." Matt turned to Dilys. "Update the team about where we are and find out if any of them have uncovered anything new, then grab us some coffee and join us."

Dilys turned away as Matt walked into his office. Aidan followed him in and plonked his bulk on the chair facing the desk. Matt hung his coat on the stand in the corner and sat.

"Been hard at it then, Aidan?" he asked.

"Yes, sir. I've been working closely with one of the NFIB's experts for the last couple of days. Clever lad, not quite twenty, but knows his way around cyberspace like no one else I've ever met." Aidan sighed heavily. "When I was his age, I was dossing around on the sofa telling everyone I was depressed. Drove my parents mad, I did."

Matt smiled. "So what changed?"

"Found myself an older woman and–" Aidan stopped speaking abruptly and his face flushed.

Matt waved away any perceived slur. "Tell me about your collaboration with the young wunderkind," he said.

Aidan nodded, opened a cardboard folder and handed two sheets of paper across the desk. "We've compiled what we believe to be a complete list of Seth Geddings' victims – those he scammed online. This was only made possible because we had access to his kit. Even then, he was careful. With the information we gleaned we could match up the known victims who had reported crimes to Action Fraud, who in turn contacted the NFIB. Many of the individuals on there didn't even report what had happened to them. People don't, you know, because they are afraid of what others will say." He snorted. "Criminals who do this sort of thing talk about a 'victimless crime' as the banks sometimes make redress, but we know there's no such thing."

"No," Matt said. "There isn't. This is quite a list. I wonder where Geddings stashed the money. I know you found that single account, but with as many crimes as this and so much money missing, there wasn't enough in there."

Matt looked up as Dilys entered with coffee and waited for her to take a seat.

"We should talk to his sister, Lois Clarke," Dilys said. "I'm sure she knows more about this than she's admitted to."

"Of course, you're right. Put it on the to-do list. I also think we need to contact everyone on *this* list. Your job, Aidan, is to find the money. This is good."

"I know," he said, "and there's more. Karen Johns spoke to me about the cabling discovered in the warehouse. My new friend has managed to track the internet traffic backwards and confirmed that some of the scams on record did in fact originate there."

"Brilliant. Dilys, ask Chloe to come in, would you?"

She nodded and went out the main office, returning a couple of minutes later with the younger officer.

"How can I help you, sir?" Chloe asked.

"Take a seat. I have a job for you. I know how good you are at researching, checking and re-checking facts for hours, and you usually get results. I'm not sure how you do it, but I'm impressed."

"Thank you, sir," she said wondering where the conversation was heading.

"Well, Aidan here – with assistance from the NFIB – has come up with a long list of individuals who he can prove were targeted by Geddings. All need looking into, whether or not they reported the crimes, the effect they might have had on them, and what they are doing now. It'll take you some time, I'm afraid."

"No problem, I enjoy this sort of stuff."

"Good, because then I want you to compile some lists of your own to include anyone who had been spoken to during previous investigations into the three murder victims. Once you've done that, and checked those individuals' histories and backgrounds, study all the lists together. We need to discover a link between these killings and I'm sure our best chance of uncovering that will be among the people who knew them. I know it's a massive task, but I also know you're up to it and that Aidan will be happy to help. Perhaps he can speed up the process somehow, write some clever algorithms or something. Make a start first thing in the morning. Any link you find, no matter how tenuous, I want to know about it."

Chloe got to her feet, nodded her agreement and left the office, Aidan behind her.

"What's our next move, sir?" Dilys asked.

"Try to tie up some of the loose ends we've collected. Set up visits with Geddings' sister and the mother of the twin girls who overdosed."

"The second visit won't be easy. Their mam won't be at all happy if we march in and stir things up again, more so because if Seddon was responsible, we have no chance of bringing him to justice."

"That's why I always appreciate having you with me, for your tact and empathy. Once you've done that, you can knock off. I need to get home earlier myself tonight. Fabia very pointedly told me she's cooking supper and expects me to be there to eat it."

* * *

As Chloe sat at her desk, her mobile rang. She smiled when she recognised her brother's number and answered the call.

"Hi, Gareth," she said. "Is everything okay with you and Theresa?"

"Yeah, everything's fine. Any chance you can meet me at the Red Dragon when you finish your shift?"

"I'm just about to leave the office, but I was planning a supermarket run. My cupboard is pretty much bare."

"You can do that tomorrow, I need to see you now. It's really important."

* * *

"This is a surprise," Chloe said. She removed her jacket and sat at a small table facing her brother. "Are you sure everything is okay at home?"

"Of course. Why wouldn't it be?"

"Because you don't often refer to an after-work drink as 'important'."

"I've had some results," Gareth said, "with that sniffing around you wanted me to do on Prendergast." He sipped from his beer glass. "I reckon I've found something."

"Have you?" Chloe leaned forward in her chair. "What have you found?"

"This morning when Prendergast came in, he logged on and got to work. Then, a few minutes later, the in-house postie knocked an entire cup of hot coffee into his lap." Gareth chuckled. "The man squealed like a stuck pig."

"I'm sorry but I don't see what this has to do with anything. And I told you I need to buy food."

"Have some patience, sis, I haven't finished. So, Prendergast shot out of the office, didn't close his computer down and" – he grinned – "while I was saving the keyboard, the documents, and wiping up the coffee, I took a peek at what he was working on. Seems I was right, he's obsessed with all things copper and especially with local murders. He's collected a massive amount of stuff directly relating to your case."

"'Stuff' is a vague term. What sort of 'stuff'?"

"Photos of the crime scenes, all three of them. There are lots of those. Some were even taken when the investigation was in progress. Photos of the white tent, your boss, and a few of the others. As I said, there's masses of it and I can't begin to imagine how he got his hands on most of it."

"Do you think he's got all that because he's working on a feature or something? Maybe it's work on his book."

"No, I reckon this is a kind of side-hustle. Honestly, you should see how much he's accumulated."

"I wish I could." Chloe sighed. "And DCI Lambert would probably kill for it."

Gareth smiled, dug into the pocket of his jeans, removed a flash drive and held it up. "Thought you'd say that, so while I was mopping, I was also copying. The file related to the murders is on there plus a couple of others. Since I had the opportunity, I copied his appointments diary and some notes too."

Chloe stared at him wide-eyed as she snatched the piece of plastic from his fingers. "Oh my God, Gareth! That's amazing. Thank you so much. Do you think Prendergast is up to something?"

"Oh, he's definitely up to something, the question is, what? I took a quick nosey at what I'd copied and the research on the victims and those around them is extensive. What gives me the creeps are the photos of the scenes and how close he must have been. I wonder if anyone working there saw him, I mean, he's a big guy and stands out."

"I wasn't there, but I'll ask around. Someone might remember him." She smiled across the table. "I can't believe you've done this for me. The boss will be chuffed to little pieces."

"That's all well and good, but if this stuff isn't relevant, you must destroy it. Also, make sure your boss knows not to chat about where this came from, because if anyone in the office thinks I'm a mole, or finds out what I've done–"

"No one will, I promise, and I'll make sure the boss keeps this quiet for now. That might change, of course, if the info proves Prendergast is a killer." She clasped his arm. "You really are lush, you know that, don't you? I think I should buy you another drink. You deserve one."

"Yes, I do." Gareth drained what was left of his beer and held out the glass, a smile on his lips.

"I'll fetch one on the way back from the loo."

Chloe walked through the bar to the toilet, locked herself in a cubicle and rang DCI Matt Lambert, who was still stuck at the station. He was surprised to hear from her, even more surprised when she swore him to secrecy and told him what Gareth had handed over. He sounded as though his birthday had arrived early.

"Gosh," he said when she finished speaking. "It sounds like Gareth has really come up trumps. Bloody good idea of yours to talk to him. Does he think Prendergast is the killer?"

"He didn't go that far, sir, and he's a reporter not a copper, but he was certainly suspicious about the amount of information the man has on our case. Everything on the drive will need looking at before we jump to any conclusions – and that will take a while."

"Yes, I agree with you, but it sounds like you've found us a new suspect. Well done, Chloe. Pass on my thanks to your brother and make sure he knows we'll keep this between ourselves for now. When you clock on tomorrow, I want you on this and let me know the second you find anything significant."

# Chapter 23

Matt walked into the warm kitchen and was pleased to see Bethan in her high chair. She stretched out her arms, waved her chubby fingers and gurgled a greeting. He walked closer, ruffled her curls until she giggled, and kissed the top of her head. Fabia looked up from the pot on the stove and smiled at her partner.

"How lovely," she said. "I was hoping you'd make it home in time, but I didn't really expect you to."

"You put me on a three-line whip, remember, so I wasn't brave enough not to be here for supper." He wrapped an arm around her waist and kissed the back of her neck.

"I should lay the law down more often. Now, pour some wine, this is nearly ready. I've made *cawl* and there's bread in the oven."

"You spoil me. I have to say this is a much better arrangement than when I used to go home to an empty apartment in town. I'm really happy we took the plunge and you allowed me to move in with you."

"Yes, me too. Things are working out well."

"I told you they would."

Matt took off his coat, opened a bottle of wine and settled at the table. His eyes were drawn the sheets of paper covered with names, colourful lines and squiggles.

"You've been busy," he said taking a closer look. "Have you managed to reach any conclusions?"

"A few, but how many are useful I'm not sure. There are so many players and I can't be sure they've all made it onto the mind map. There are bound to be some no one even knows about. How have you got on today? Made any progress?"

She opened the oven, placed the freshly baked loaf on the table next to a block of locally made butter, then filled bowls with rich lamb broth. As they ate their meal, Matt brought Fabia up to date with the investigation and told her about the lists Chloe would be tackling in the morning.

"I'll give her your mind map, it's bound to help," he said.

"That young woman is shaping up to be an excellent officer," Fabia said. "She'll go far, that one, mark my words."

"I think you're right there." Matt wiped a hunk of bread around his bowl and crammed it into his mouth. "I had a word with Erica before I left work. Like me, she is sure the Michaelsons know much more than they are saying, so I'm going to have a couple of uniforms stake the place out. We know next to nothing about what they get up to, where they go and who they visit, so that has to be worth a go."

"That's a good idea. Was Erica okay with it?"

"Yes. Even though an operation like that will suck money from the budget, she's sanctioned it for the next few days. Twenty-four-hour surveillance. She'll monitor the situation but agrees it has to be worth a try." He drained his glass. "Right then, I'll put our chick to bed then you talk me through your conclusions."

When Matt came back downstairs Fabia had taken their glasses and moved into the living room where she had lit the fire.

"Did she go down?" she asked.

"Yes, almost immediately once I'd tucked her in and wound up the mobile she likes so much. She's such a contented little girl, must take after her mother." Matt sat on the sofa next to Fabia. "Now, tell me about your discoveries."

"Not really discoveries of the hard facts you like," she said, "more intuition, feelings." She leaned forward and pointed at the diagrams on the paper spread on the coffee table. "It occurred to me that there are women involved with all these murdered men, women who have been badly treated, suffered because of the men's actions. The ones Geddings scammed, those who were stalked by Prosser, and of course the two young women who died and their mother, more than likely because of the drugs manufactured by Seddon. It seems to me they all had good reasons to want to see their tormenters dead."

"Are you suggesting the killer we seek is female?"

"I think you should give the possibility more thought."

"Would a woman be able to physically capture a man, torture him, then dump the body? Not once, but three times? I'm not saying a woman wouldn't have the will to do these things, but how would she control a bigger, stronger man? Are you suggesting the aggrieved women worked together?"

"I'm not suggesting anything. I'm just saying your team should look at the investigations in a different way, not rule anything out because the solution is unlikely or uncomfortable. I'm a firm believer that anyone can achieve pretty much anything if they have the will and the determination. You've heard the saying 'there's more than one way to skin a cat'."

"Yes, I understand, and Dilys has said much the same thing. I'll make the point tomorrow at the briefing."

"Also bear in mind what we've said when you speak to Mrs Saunders tomorrow. Try to put yourself in her place, imagine what she could be capable of. That is not going to be an easy conversation."

"No, it won't. I'm not looking forward to it and I'm very glad I'll have Dilys with me." Matt put his arm around Fabia's shoulders. "Thank you for doing this, it's useful stuff. I told Erica Talbot I'd discussed the case with you and she sounded pleased to have you onboard – even in an unofficial capacity. Said some very complimentary things about you." Matt leaned in and kissed Fabia soundly. "Let's Netflix and chill," he said. "Take advantage of Bethan being asleep."

"Good idea. You make the popcorn, I'll find something good to watch."

* * *

The team gathered the next morning and Matt stood beneath the whiteboard displaying details of the multilayered investigation. He waited as they settled then delivered the briefing, told his officers where he wanted them to look, and assigned tasks. He informed DC Sara Gupta and PC Craig Evans that they would be staking out the flat where the Michaelsons lived. PC Karim Singh and DC Becca Pryce would handle the night shift.

"We need to know about their movements," he said. "Where they go, who they speak to and how they spend their days. Keep notes and keep your heads down. I don't want them to know they are being watched. The rest of you who are not involved with the paperwork, get out onto the street, talk to local people, try to find any potential witnesses, and of course keep your ears open. Gossip nearly always contains a speck of truth and we might learn something. Chloe will be working with Aidan checking through the lists of those effected by the actions of the murdered men, and looking for the link that must be there. If we can find that link then we should make significant progress clearing up these crimes. Dilys and I will be out of the office, we have a couple of interviews to conduct and hopefully, they will provide a useful thread or two." He shrugged into his jacket. "If any one of you discovers anything that might be useful, don't keep it to yourselves and let me know immediately. We have to make more progress on this and stop spinning our wheels. On with it, then."

Dilys moved closer to stand next to him. "Who shall we speak to first, sir?" she asked.

"Lisa Saunders, the mother of the twins. Be good to get the most difficult task out of the way first. Then we'll have another word with Lois Clarke, the sister of Geddings. Tell me, have we been able to trace any relatives of Sky Laska, the young woman who committed suicide, due in part to the actions of Prosser?"

"No, sir. Chloe and I have been looking but have come to the conclusion that any family she has are not in the country. We've been able to discover she came to Wales from Poland, attended Bangor University and subsequently got a job at a call centre. She rented a small flat but lived alone."

"No friends?" Matt asked.

"If there were, we haven't been able to find any. She was just the sort of woman Prosser picked on – lonely without much in the way of backup."

"Okay but we need to keep at it. Have one of the team make enquiries where she came from, as well as speaking to the university she attended and the company she worked for. There must be something."

"Yes, sir."

"Go and round up a car and I'll meet you out the back as soon as I've let Erica Talbot know what we're up to."

* * *

A short while later, Matt went out to the car park and got in the passenger seat of an unmarked, dark-blue Mondeo. Dilys started the engine and set off for the outskirts of Newport where Lisa Saunders, mother of

Casey and Carys, lived. She threaded her way through town and once out of the traffic made good progress. She pulled up outside a row of brick-built terraced houses, with small front gardens, evergreen hedges and a few daffodils growing in pots. Cars were parked at intervals along the street, and an old man plodded along the road with a scruffy-looking mongrel on a lead. A couple of mothers pushed strollers, both tapping at their phones. Dilys turned off the engine and turned to face her boss.

"I'm not looking forward to this, sir," she said. "We have to be very gentle with her, she had a bit of a breakdown when her girls died and we don't want to upset her or make her ill again."

Matt grimaced. "I know, which is why I want you to take the lead. Not only are you good at encouraging people to talk, you always take the time to understand how they are feeling." He opened the door. "Let's get this over with then."

They walked up to the red front door, rang the bell and waited until a small, pretty woman, with dark hair and pale skin peered out.

Dilys introduced them and they both displayed their warrant cards. "Good morning, Ms Saunders, thank you for agreeing to speak to us."

Lisa Saunders sighed. "I didn't feel I had much choice. I'll put the kettle on. Difficult conversations always tend to go better with tea, don't you think?"

"I do. Thank you," Dilys said.

Dilys and Matt followed the woman along a short, narrow hall and into a small kitchen at the rear of the property. The officers sat at the little table as their host made tea. Then she placed steaming mugs in front of them.

"So, how do you think I can help you?" Lisa asked.

"We weren't involved with the original investigation regarding the death of your girls," Dilys began, "so perhaps you could start by telling us about them, and about the time they died. I know this will be difficult for you, so please take your time."

Lisa nodded and gulped from her mug. "I'll be straight with you here," she said, "I've been dreading your visit. Most of the time I can screw on a face that the world finds acceptable, so I can move between other people, but I'm not one of them anymore. I'm the woman who was careless enough to lose twin girls." She took a deep breath. "Born on the same day and died on the same day."

Tears welled in her eyes and Lisa suddenly broke down and sobbed loudly. Dilys reached out to touch her shoulder. "Don't!" the woman warned. "If you give me any sympathy, I won't be any use to you."

Dilys withdrew her hand and waited for the spasm of grief to pass.

Matt's eyebrows were deeply furrowed and his heart ached for this wounded mother. A sudden thought entered his mind and he wondered how he would feel if he lost Bethan. A violent shudder passed through his body. He gritted his teeth against it and waited for Lisa to continue. He knew she had more to say and watched as she took a deep, calming breath before she began to speak.

"All their lives, it was just the three of us against the world," she eventually said. "The lad who got me pregnant scarpered as soon as he heard I was expecting." She wiped her eyes. "Their birth was difficult. There were complications, for them and me, and we nearly didn't make it. The staff were brilliant, though, and we were lucky. I brought them up alone. My parents are devout Christians and once I'd told them I was pregnant, I became a loose woman in their eyes and they abandoned me."

"Must have been incredibly tough," Dilys said.

Lisa smiled weakly. "You have no idea. We managed, and things got better. My beautiful girls grew up and went to school. They were clever – both of them. I got a job, saved hard and eventually we bought this little house." She gazed up at the ceiling. "We were happy here, the three of us, and just when they were ready to go out into the world and begin their own lives, they were taken from me." More tears began to fall. "I'll never forget them."

"Of course you won't," Dilys said, "nor should you. I am very sorry for your loss, truly I am."

"Yes, I can tell. Thank you." She wiped her face, blew her nose and sat up straighter in her seat. "Now we've got that out of the way, please tell me why you are here."

"During the original investigation," Dilys said, "you probably know the police spoke to a local man who was suspected of manufacturing the drugs your daughters took."

Lisa's face turned hard, grey like stone. "Seddon!" she spat. "Jake Seddon. He got away with what he'd done. How was it possible that he was allowed to walk away after the damage he'd caused?"

"As Sergeant Bevin said, he was spoken to at the time, but no matter how hard we dug into his background and his activities, we were never able to find enough evidence for an arrest warrant, never mind enough to convince the CPS we had a case," Matt replied. "Seddon was clever and covered his tracks well."

Lisa sat forward in her seat. "Was? You said 'was'."

Matt nodded. "His body was discovered in the old Usk railway tunnel. You may have read about the case. He was murdered."

For a moment, the unhappy woman didn't blink. It seemed as though an eternity passed before she began making a strange choking sound, somewhere between laughing and howling. She struggled for air and Dilys filled a glass with water. Lisa snatched it gratefully and guzzled, water escaping from her lips to run down her chin. "Oh my," she mumbled repeatedly, before finally looking up at Matt.

"Did he suffer?" she asked. "Please, tell me he did. That his death was not an easy one. It was a deserved one. That bastard took my babies' lives – and my own. He took everything from me. I hope he's burning in hell. Do you know who killed him?"

"Not yet and that's why we wanted to speak to you."

Lisa blinked. "Do you think I killed him?"

"No, madam, but we need to speak to all those who were affected by his actions, as well as all those who knew him."

"But I was on the top of your list. Well, I'll tell you plainly I didn't murder the man. I'm glad someone did, I fully admit that, but it wasn't me – more's the pity. If I'd ever had the opportunity, met him out one night with a gun in my hand, I wouldn't have hesitated to blow his head off his shoulders, but I was never in that position. Can you tell me how he was killed? There wasn't very much in the paper about the body found in the tunnel."

"I'm sorry, Lisa," Dilys said. "Because our investigation is still ongoing, we can't tell you much, but there were clear signs he had been attacked and the injuries he sustained caused his death."

"There will be a case in the Coroner's Court, though, won't there?"

"Yes, that will take place in due course."

"Would you tell me when that happens? I'd like to be there."

"Of course we will," Dilys said. "Do you happen to know whether any of Casey and Cary's friends were affected at the same time? Did you keep in contact with anyone else involved?"

Lisa shook her head. "I never really knew that group of friends, and after my girls died, I shut myself away. I'm afraid I wouldn't be able to help you there."

Dilys nodded. "Do you have any idea who might have wanted Seddon dead?"

"No one I know of, apart from me."

"Could you tell us where you were from about five o'clock on Thursday last week?" Matt said gently.

Lisa frowned and tapped a finger against her cheek. "I would have been at work till six," she said. "And then I would have been here. Why? Wasn't the body in the tunnel found at the beginning of the week?"

Matt nodded but didn't answer the question.

"Would you mind having a look at these pictures to see if you recognise these men?" Dilys said. She tilted her iPad around to show Lisa the pictures of Seth Geddings and Huw Prosser.

Lisa shrugged. "No, sorry."

Matt nodded and got to his feet. "Okay, thank you for speaking with us. I understand how hard it must have been and I am sorry for the distress we have caused. Will you be okay? Is there someone who could sit with you for a while?"

Lisa wiped her eyes. "I'll be fine. I've become very good at self-sufficiency over the years. Thank you though for bringing me the news of that monster's death, and good luck with your investigation."

Lisa Saunders showed her guests out and closed the door behind them.

"That poor woman," Dilys said when they were in the car. "Those who lose children never recover. It's wrong when the young die before the old, it's not the right order of things, is it?"

"No, it isn't. I'm sure that if anything bad happened to Bethan I wouldn't be able to keep breathing."

Matt looked so disturbed by the thought that Dilys placed a hand on his arm. "Nothing will happen to Bethan, sir. You and Fabia will keep her safe, I know you will."

Matt nodded and scrubbed at his eyes. "Okay then, let's head over to Sketty for that chat with Lois Clarke. We need to try and squeeze out anything she knows about her brother's activities. We never really got to the bottom of what caused the family rift."

# Chapter 24

Dilys parked the car in Vivian Road outside a row of three-storey, Victorian houses. Each had large bay windows, and the upper floors were mock-Tudor – black and white timbered.

"Nice place, sir," Dilys said as she left the car. "Expensive too for Sketty. I'm not sure I'd like rattling around on my own in a place as big as this."

"Perhaps she rents out rooms," Matt suggested.

"Nothing like that mentioned during her previous interview. I think she told the local officers who spoke to her that she was in PR. I'm not entirely sure what that means she does, but presumably she's good at it to afford such a place."

Matt nodded and led the way up a short flight of steep steps to the front door, rang the bell and heard it clang loudly inside. After a short wait, a middle-aged woman opened the door. She was very smartly dressed in a pastel skirt and jacket, a thick rope of pearls at her neck, and designer shoes on her feet.

"You must be the police," she said and glanced at a gold wristwatch. "You're late and I don't appreciate being kept waiting." She studied their warrant cards and opened the door wider. "Well, you're here now, so let's get on with it. I have another appointment shortly. Go straight on through to the kitchen."

Dilys set off along the hall, Matt behind her. They walked into a large and airy room that looked as though it could have appeared in the pages of a *Homes & Gardens* magazine. On one wall was a large stove with a polished copper hood above. Granite worktops stretched away from each edge and within one was nestled a deep stone sink with shiny taps. On the far end of the room was a picture window looking out onto a beautifully kept garden.

"You have a lovely home, Ms Clarke," Dilys said. "I've always wanted a kitchen like this. It's probably bigger than the ground floor of my house."

The well-dressed woman smiled proudly. "It suits me," she said. "Please, do sit down. Can I fetch you something to drink?"

"No, thank you, madam," Matt said and took a seat at a highly polished table.

Lois Clarke settled herself opposite him as Dilys removed her tablet from its case and placed it on the surface.

"I'd like to record our conversation, if you have no objections," she said.

"None at all." Lois chuckled softly. "Seems police officers with pocketbooks are a thing of the past. Now, what can I do for you? I'm assuming you want to talk about my brother, Seth."

"Yes, that's right," Dilys said. "We are sorry for your loss and apologise for having to disturb you at this time."

"No matter, we all have our jobs to do and I would like to help you catch his killer. It's difficult to obtain closure with so many unanswered questions hanging over the issue." She glanced at her watch a second time. "I have to remind you though, we don't have long."

"We'll be as quick as we can. When you spoke to local officers, you told them of an instance when your brother had been seen in Usk by an old school friend of yours. Is that correct?"

Lois nodded. "Yes, that's right. We had lost contact a while ago so it was heartening to know he was still in the land of the living."

"Did you try to track him down or contact him?"

"No, we were estranged."

"We've been told by a man who rented him a room that there had been some sort of falling out between Seth and the family. Can you tell us what caused that?"

Lois took a deep breath. "It was all very silly, really. Seth dropped out of university and our parents were very angry about it. They had paid the tuition fees for him and have always hated wasting money. There was a huge row at the time when it became obvious he had no intention of returning, and ties were severed."

"Had you spoken to him since that happened?"

"Once. A couple of years ago, I arranged for us to have lunch together, neutral ground you see? I made a mistake of taking Mother with me, and I have to say it didn't go as I had hoped."

"Why was that?" Matt asked.

"I'd booked an expensive restaurant in one of the hotels on the edge of town. Seth was late and when he eventually turned up it looked as though he had slept in his clothes. I'm surprised he was allowed in. Mother was horrified and wanted to leave, but I calmed her down and we ordered. Honestly, I was shaken by the change in him."

"How had he changed?"

"He'd turned from a smart young man into a scruffy hippy-type, with a skinhead haircut and tattoos on his neck and forearms – just awful. As I said, Mother was shocked. I knew then that he wouldn't be welcomed back into the fold." She gazed up at the ceiling. "Thank God I didn't take Father with us, he would have caused an awful scene, I know he would." She looked at Matt. "Why does anyone throw their life away like that?"

"You don't have any idea?" he asked.

"Sadly no, but he had the best chances in life. He could have made something of himself like I have."

"You seem to have done very well."

"Hard work and determination. Two qualities lacking in my brother, I'm sorry to say."

"So, that was the last time you spoke to him?" Dilys asked.

"Yes. He never got in touch and I knew he was a lost cause. I don't waste my time on lost causes, never have."

"You have said you work in PR?"

Lois smiled. "I *own* a successful PR company. These days others do the work. I keep a steady hand on the tiller and reap the benefits. Now, if there's nothing else, I really do have to get on. There's never enough hours in the day, is there?" She got to her feet.

"One last thing," said Dilys. She showed the pictures of Jake Seddon and Huw Prosser to Lois.

"No, never seen either of them before, I'm afraid," said Lois. "Now, if we're done, I really ought to get on."

They left the kitchen and Lois showed Matt and Dilys to the door. "One thing though," she said, "do you know when it might be possible to arrange my brother's funeral? My parents are anxious to know."

"We'll be in touch," Matt said. "Thank you for your time."

As they walked back to the car Dilys asked, "What exactly is PR, sir?"

"My understanding is bigging someone up to sound better than they are so they can make money." He glanced at his watch. "Yes, time is getting on, we need to be at the station to review the evidence we've collected so far. We're missing something somewhere."

"Rightio, sir. Should we interview Geddings' parents?"

"I'm not sure we'd learn anything new, but we will if it becomes necessary. We should contact them, regardless."

* * *

The office was busy when Matt and Dilys arrived. Many of the desks were occupied as officers stared at screens or bent over mounds of paperwork. Matt spotted Aidan and Chloe working together and walked towards them.

"How are you getting on?" he asked. "Making any progress?"

"It's slow work, sir," Chloe said. "We've nearly finished compiling the lists you asked for and Aidan is working on an algorithm to make the comparison tasks easier. I still haven't been able to track anyone connected to Sky Laska. I think the only way I'll be able to make progress will be to contact the police in Poland. I wanted to check with you before."

Matt frowned. "Okay, leave it with me and of course, speak to the authorities in Poland. I'm not sure how you will explain the delay in contacting them, but if it all gets too difficult just refer them to me."

"Yes, sir, thank you."

Matt looked at her pointedly. "What about…?"

"It's in hand, sir."

"Aidan," Matt said. "I want you to look into the finances of Lois Clarke. Dilys and I spoke to her today and she's not short of a bob or two. She lives in a large house in Sketty and the place is like a palace inside, no expense spared. She told us she owns a 'successful PR company' so I'd like you to take a look at that. Any sniff of bad or dubious behaviour, I want to know."

"Of course, I'll get right on it."

Matt went to his office and had barely sat down when there was a tap on the door. He looked up as Sara Gupta and Craig Evans entered.

"Is it that time already?" he asked.

"Yes, sir," Sara said. "We've handed over the surveillance to Karim and Becca and came to give you our report before we knock off."

Matt waved them to chairs. "Let's hear it then."

Sara took out her notebook and flipped pages. Matt smiled, recalling Lois Clarke's comment.

"They don't seem to do much, sir," she said, "mainly hang around in the flat all day, watching crap on telly I reckon, although the boy is probably messing about online, gaming, social media or whatever. At 11.43 Cari Michaelson left home and went to the local supermarket." Sara snorted derisively. "She was dressed in her jim-jams. I followed her while Craig stayed outside the flat."

"I thought the supermarkets had banned customers from wearing their pyjamas when they shopped," Matt said.

His young officer smiled. "They did, sir. Quite the thing in Merthyr for a while. Seems as though Cari hasn't got the message. Anyway" – she consulted her notes – "she bought ready meals, cans of lager, a fair amount of junk food, crisps, stuff like that, and cigarettes, then toddled back home. She didn't leave home again before we handed over to the next team."

"What about her boy, Paul? Did he go anywhere?"

Craig took up the story. "Not until later in the afternoon, just before 4.30. He visited the corner shop, bought a small bag of groceries, a local paper and some milk, then called at a ground floor flat in the next block over. An older woman answered the door. I've checked council records and the resident is Ena Michaelson, mother of Cari and grandmother of the two boys. He stayed about an hour, then left the flat and went back home. Again, he didn't go anywhere else before we left." He huffed. "Bit of a boring day all round really, sir."

"No one called at their place?" Matt asked.

"No, sir."

"Okay, thanks for that. Write it up before you leave so I can copy the boss in, then take the day shift tomorrow and we'll see what that turns up."

"Maybe they are night owls," Sara said.

"Hopefully the second team will be able to prove or disprove that. Good job, both of you."

The officers got to their feet and left, closing the door behind them.

Another hour passed before Matt stretched and leaned back in his chair. It had felt like a very long day and he groaned. Most of his team had already left for the day and he knew he should have headed for home a while ago. He also knew Fabia wouldn't be best pleased if he was late again, but since talking to Lisa Saunders, a black mood had descended on him. He was sure his partner would spot it and ask questions but he didn't want to tell her what was bothering him. He knew it was his problem not hers and didn't want to pass on the fear that had settled in his heart, and was the reason he had remained at his desk reading the mountain of reports the investigation had generated.

The thickest file on his desk had come from Chloe, one of the hardest workers on his team. The first document he examined related to a phone call she had made to the Polish police. He was impressed because soon after her call, they had been able to trace a family member of Sky Laska's. She was eventually able to speak to Sky's grandmother who had brought the girl up following the death of her parents at a young age, and was still very upset about her granddaughter's untimely death. Unfortunately, she was unable to provide any new information. Chloe had added a note on how useful her training in family liaison had been.

The other reports in the files were the lists she had compiled with Aidan's assistance. Matt sucked in his breath when he saw how many names the lists contained. One list however was notable for being more or less empty. Only two names appeared below that of Prosser – those of Sky and Cath Temple. Matt rubbed his eyes. How was it possible that anyone could move through life without collecting some friends and associates? Chloe had added a few more notes.

> No previous or current work history. Bank account opened

> when he moved to the area. Looks like he was hiding – or someone was hiding him.

Matt frowned at the last comment and the germ of an idea began swirling in the back of his mind, but he couldn't snag the notion and bring it to the front. He decided he was tired and it was time to call it a day and face the music at home.

He reached out to switch off his computer just as a message pinged in. He was tempted to ignore it, but sat back in his chair and saw that Karen Johns had sent an e-mail. The heading read, 'Early report on items recovered from the Michaelsons' warehouse'. He hoped it contained some good news to take home with him, held his breath and opened the e-mail.

# Chapter 25

At eight the next morning, Matt stood beneath the incident board at the end of the room. He buttoned his jacket as Erica Talbot entered and moved to stand next to a wall, and two constables shifted slightly to make a space.

"Okay then," he said. "Listen up."

He took a couple of breaths as the room quietened and all heads turned towards him. "Last night I received an e-mail from Karen Johns at SOCO. The bad news is that the bloodstains on the floor are not a match to any of our victims."

There was a groan from the team and Matt raised his hand to silence them.

"The good news is," he continued, "that she collected DNA samples from the cable found at the Michaelsons' warehouse, as well as further samples from the sink area at the back of the building and the toilet. She has been able to confirm that among the samples she took, one was an exact match to Jake Seddon and another to Paul Michaelson. We already know Geddings used the warehouse from Aidan's good work before." Matt lifted his eyes. "What that means, among other things, is that Paul lied to us. He had been there. I want to know why he lied, what he's hiding, how involved he was with Seddon and Geddings, and discover the link with Prosser. There must be one somewhere."

He took a sip from a bottle of water. "This boy is guilty of something, quite possibly murder, and I want to gather enough evidence to reduce the likelihood of him escaping justice to zero. So, we double down on the surveillance of him and his mam, every minute of every day I want someone watching. Chief Superintendent Talbot is obtaining permission to monitor their phones and internet usage. While that is underway, Sergeant Bevan and I will visit Dai Michaelson again. I want to know whether or not he is directing his brother's activities and the previous interview told us nothing."

"What's stopping him lying to us, sir?" an officer at the back of the room asked.

"Nothing, but I'm hoping he will want to avoid adding more years to his already lengthy sentence on a charge of perverting the course of justice in a triple homicide."

He glanced up towards Aidan. "What have you discovered about Lois Clarke?"

"On paper, she is what she says she is," Aidan said. "A successful businesswoman, running a successful PR company, for successful clients who pay shed loads of money for her services. I think there's more to find though."

"Make sure you let me know the second you have anything. Meanwhile, I'll arrange for Swansea nick to keep an inconspicuous eye on her. Now, before we crack on, CS Talbot would like a word. Ma'am?"

Erica nodded, walked to the front of the room and stood beside Matt.

"Good morning, all of you. I won't take up too much of your time, I know you have a busy few days in front of you. As you will be aware, the press is having a field day with this, but I know we can't wave magic wands and solve such a difficult case as quickly as they would like."

She cast her eyes around the room. "What I don't want is any mistakes being made. The person who killed three men in our area must not be allowed to get away with it, we must catch them. By the book, boys and girls, by the book." She looked around and saw nodding heads. "I know you are tired, but the team has made good progress with the investigation and we have enough evidence to take to court as soon as a suspect is in custody. We need one good push forward now and I know I can count on you. Thank you."

For a moment, Matt wondered whether the officers would applaud, but they resisted. He liked Erica, admired her as his boss, and knew the team appreciated her hands-on approach – very different to what they had been used to. He showed her from the room, then turned back to his team.

"You all heard what the governor said, so get out there and do your best work. Be back here at close of business for debriefing. We must get on top of this now."

Matt watched as some officers left the room with an air of positivity, while others returned to their desks and began trawling the evidence.

Dilys approached him. "You said we were visiting Dai Michaelson?" she asked.

"Yes, I've been onto the prison and they are expecting us. I'll take the lead in the interview – we need to push him much harder." He grinned. "I have been working on my bad cop persona."

Dilys raised her eyebrows. "Have you, sir? Where do I come in?"

"It will be you who throws him a crumb and makes him *want* to talk to us. Right, let's get downstairs and we'll make tracks."

"Sir?"

Matt turned. "Yes, Chloe?"

"I know you are on your way out, but I could really do with a quick word – about that stuff you wanted."

"Okay, but it will have to be quick." He looked at Dilys. "I'll meet you downstairs," he said.

"Take a seat, Chloe," Matt said when they'd returned to his office, "and tell me what you have."

"I've been wading through the stuff on that flash drive and I'm horrified how much Prendergast knows about our investigation. Those pictures at the scenes are worrying. He managed to get really close when SOCO was there, but no one remembers seeing him and he was never spoken to. There are more pictures taken without the white tent and the circus. They worry me because I can't work out whether they were taken pre- or post-tent, if you see what I mean. Usually, digital cameras have a time stamp that saves when the image was taken but he's disguised it. All the pictures say they were taken at different times in the year 2049. Obviously, it would make a huge difference and I keep thinking there must be some way to work it out but…"

Matt smiled. It usually took Chloe longer to run out of words.

"I can see where you're going with this. Can you show me some pictures?"

"Yes, sir, I have an example."

Chloe placed her laptop on his desk and tapped the keyboard. Two side-by-side images of the Usk tunnel appeared on the screen.

"See what I mean? If we could work out when the picture without the tent was taken, it might give us a lead, especially if it was *before* the body was found."

Matt peered at the screen. "You're right Chloe, this is good work. When I was a kid there were puzzles in comics called 'Spot the Difference'. Have a chat with Aidan, maybe he'll be able to run some sort of comparison? Compare the brambles or something." He smiled again. "You might be onto something here."

"Thank you, sir, and there's something else."

Matt raised his eyebrows.

"I've been working my way through Prendergast's appointments diary and I've noticed something." She tapped the keyboard again and called up a new screen. "He has contact with plenty of people and it will take some time to work through them all with background checks and such, but immediately after the first body was found a new name appeared and Prendergast has been visiting that person regularly ever since." She pointed to an entry in the digital diary and Matt rubbed his eyes in disbelief.

"Gosh," he said, "this puts a different light on things. Leave it with me, I'll need a little while to think this through properly. Not a word to anybody, okay? We'll speak again when Dilys and I return from the prison."

"Yes, sir."

* * *

Following an hour of having their photos taken, enduring pat-downs by enthusiastic prison officers, and checking in the majority of their belongings at the desk, Matt and Dilys were finally shown to the small interview room. A short while later, Dai Michaelson was brought in. He shuffled to the desk and dropped onto the empty plastic chair.

"Don't you have anything better to do?" he asked. "Don't get me wrong, twenty-three hour bang-up is hard, so a while out of the cell is always welcome, but you seem to have a bit of a thing for me." He winked at Dilys. "Is that what it is, my lovely? You've seen my mug shot and have got the hots for me?"

Dilys said nothing but looked him in the eye.

"You can pack that in right now," Matt said. "It won't help your cause in any way."

Dai snorted. "I don't have a cause. There's nothing you can do to me while I'm in here, serving my sentence. When I get to the end, I'll be let out. Not so long to go now and I'm looking forward to being back on the streets."

"If I have my way," Matt growled, "your release date will keep moving into the future."

"Yeah, course it will. Do you see me quaking in my boots?" He leaned back in his chair and folded his arms across his belly. "Better tell me what you want then? I have a busy schedule."

"Your brother has been lying to us."

"And why does that have anything to do with me?"

"Because we believe you are still running your gang from inside these walls, and your brother is acting on orders from you."

Dai threw back his head and laughed. "Prove it! You can't, can you? You come here with daft questions" – he gazed at Dilys with a twisted smile on his face – "not that I'm complaining about the view. Not much worth looking at in here and certainly nothing as lovely as your sergeant."

Matt slapped the tabletop and made everyone in the room jump. "I have told you, Michaelson, I want no more of that. I want you to tell me what your brother has to do with the deaths of three men close to Newport."

"What you want and what I can tell you are two different things. I can't tell you what I don't know."

Matt tried a different tack. "Tell us why your brother has been inside your warehouse. We know, and can prove, he was there, yet he and his mother both insist they've never been there."

"How do I know what's going on outside? If you say they were there and can prove it, then good on you, but I can't say anything about it because I wasn't there."

"This is your only chance, Dai," Dilys said. "I know my boss and when he walks out of here, he will move heaven and earth to have you convicted for perverting the course of justice. In a triple murder like this, you could be looking at life."

Dai shook his head and looked at his hands.

"Don't test him," she warned. "He can make things very difficult for you in here, and for your mam and brother. Just tell him, did Paul use the warehouse? Was he working for you?"

Dai didn't reply and Matt suddenly surged to his feet. "This is a waste of time, Sergeant," he said. "We know what's been going on and have the evidence, we don't really need him to say anything. Still" – he caught the prisoner's eye and sent him a wink of his own – "at least he'll be off the streets until after I retire. He'll be someone else's problem then."

Dilys gazed across the table at Dai who suddenly didn't seem so cocky. "He'll do it," she said. "If you really don't know anything about the murders, didn't order your brother to carry them out, now's the time to tell us. Is it possible that Paul is the killer?"

For a while no one spoke or moved, then Dai groaned, leaned forward on the table and rubbed his face.

"Paul's not a killer," he said. "I don't want him locked up. He doesn't do well in prison."

"Then tell us what he's been up to," Dilys said quietly. "Do yourself a favour."

"I hear whispers on the wing," Dai said eventually. "Nothing about murder. Maybe something about Paul though."

"What did you hear?"

Dai groaned again. "Paul has been involved in some minor stuff. I don't know all the details as he hasn't spoken to me about any of it himself."

"Tell us the details you did hear," Matt growled across the table. "I'm losing my patience."

"Minor stuff, like I said. He sells cheap baccy from Europe, I think he has a small protection racket on the go, and someone in here once told me he rents out my warehouse on the industrial estate."

"What for?" Matt demanded.

"No idea. Paul's never mentioned anything about it to me, and I can't even be sure the guy in here wasn't winding me up."

"What's the guy's name?"

Dai smiled. "John. Don't know his last name and he was released months ago."

"Convenient," Matt muttered darkly.

"Can't help that, can I? It's what happened."

Dilys placed three photographs of the murdered men on the table. "Do you don't recognise anyone in these pictures? Have you ever come across any of them, alone or with your brother?"

Dai shrugged and pointed to the photo of Seddon. "I knew Jake from years back, husband of my cousin Gwyneth. We did business once upon a time."

"What kind of business?"

"I sold him a car." Dai leaned back in his seat. "I don't know the others and that is the truth."

"So, if Paul didn't kill these men, do you know who did?"

"Nope. I just know it wasn't my brother. He doesn't have it in him."

* * *

When the officers got back to the car, Matt leaned on the roof and gazed up at the sky.

"Do you think he's telling the truth, Dilys?" he asked.

"Could be. You certainly rattled him with your bad cop act, so yes, maybe. I'm not sure I can see Paul as a killer either. Nasty little scumbag, but murdering people with intent? I'm really not sure."

"We can prove he was in the warehouse though, even if we know that wasn't the site of the murders, that links him to Seddon and Geddings. When we get back to the station I'll have a word with the boss, find out what she thinks. My opinion is that we should have him back in, confront him with what we've got and what we know, maybe infer Dai has told us something, and who knows? Paul may just confess."

They got into the car and Dilys started the engine, reversed out of the space and headed for the exit. The best part of an hour later they arrived outside the station and Matt headed upstairs in search of Erica Talbot. She was in her office and waved him in when he tapped on her open door.

"Take a seat," she said. "How did it go at the prison?"

"We made some limited progress," Matt said. He told her what they'd found out. "Dai insists his brother isn't a killer, but I'm not so sure. Have there been any results from the wiretaps?"

"Bit too early yet, but Aidan has been monitoring the internet and mobile use and confirms Paul does seem to have a gang around him. They look like runners, so perhaps he is dealing as well."

"Do you think we have enough to bring him in?"

Erica leaned back in her chair. "Yes, I think we do. We have the DNA evidence and proof he lied to us during interview. Now it seems he has been renting out the warehouse, and we know, and can prove, a link to two of our victims. An arrest warrant won't be too difficult to obtain and then we'll have the opportunity to search his place and seize his digital equipment. With a bit of luck Aidan will then be able to find more hard evidence."

"So you want us to arrest him?"

"I don't think we have anywhere else to go."

"Actually, ma'am, we might have another avenue."

Erica raised her eyebrows and listened carefully as Matt told her about the new line of inquiry. He was grateful she didn't ask where the new information came from. He knew that should it lead to an arrest and if sufficient, legitimate evidence was gathered, it might not matter.

"So how do you propose to handle this?" she asked.

"Prendergast is meeting his contact tomorrow afternoon. I'll put a couple of the team on his tail. I want to ensure the entries in the diary are correct, rather than fiction, before we even think about making arrests."

"That sounds reasonable, but I thought you were on a day off on Thursday."

"I am, technically, but I'm not far away." He got to his feet. "Anyway, as I said, this is reconnaissance only at this stage. I'm minded to put the arrest of Paul Michaelson on the back burner until we've looked at this properly."

Erica nodded. "Yes, do that. We've got Paul and Cari under surveillance, so if there's any sign of flight, we can nab them."

# Chapter 26

Matt was about to put a chunk of roast potato in his mouth when his mobile rang. Fabia frowned.

"On reflection," she said, "I think I was happier when you forgot to charge the blessed thing."

Matt leaned over and peered at the device. "I'm sorry, my love, it's work. I'll have to take it." He swiped the screen and put it on speakerphone. "DCI Lambert."

"Sorry to disturb you, sir. Craig Evans here."

"So now you have, what have you got to tell me?"

"We're in the Mumbles, sir, me and Sara Gupta. We followed Prendergast like you said. We lost him for a little while, but as we knew where he was going, it was easy to pick him up again. He's just arrived at Gwyn's place."

"You mean, ex-Detective Sergeant Jones?"

Matt saw Fabia glare at him across the table, her eyes full of questions.

"Yes, sir. Anyway, Prendergast went inside and a couple of minutes later Gwyn came out."

"Did he go anywhere?"

"No, sir. He opened the boot of a car on the drive and…" Matt heard Craig take a deep breath. "He's only lifted out a bloody wheelchair!"

Matt drew in a breath of his own. "Are you sure?"

"No doubt. What do you want us to do now? What if he's planning another murder?"

"Stay where you are. Do not take your eyes off the place and keep your heads down. I don't want him spooked. I'm leaving now and I'll bring some backup."

Matt hung up and looked across the table at Fabia. "That was PC Evans. He's just seen Gwyn Jones carry a wheelchair into his house."

"Yes, I heard."

"I hate to say this, my love, but it seems as though your intuition needs retuning."

"I don't know what you are talking about." Fabia stared at him wide-eyed. "Gwyn can't be involved in the killings. I told you, he'd never do something so dreadful, I know he wouldn't."

Matt shrugged and got to his feet. "We can all make mistakes, and I'm sorry about this, but I have to go."

"Why were you even looking at Gwyn? You never said anything to me."

"Some new information came in…"

"Which you didn't share."

"I promise we'll talk later, but I really have to go."

He ruffled Bethan's curls and kissed her forehead, brushed a second kiss on Fabia's cheek, who appeared not to notice, then grabbed his jacket, phone and keys. In the car, he rang Dilys and told her he would pick her up.

* * *

An hour later, Matt and Dilys left their car and walked slowly along the street, anxious not to draw attention to themselves. A couple of squad cars were parked further away, the drivers told to keep out of sight until Matt called them in. He hoped they wouldn't be needed. Reaching the car containing DC Sara Gupta and PC Craig Evans, Matt quietly opened the back door and he and Dilys slipped inside.

"Any movement?" he asked.

"No, sir," Sara said. "No one in or out."

"Just the pair of them inside?"

"Haven't seen anyone else since we've been here." Craig nodded towards a dark vehicle parked close to the house. "That's the journalist's car, the Toyota."

"We reckon they are in the front room," Sara said. "Every now and again, we see one of them move past the window."

"And you definitely saw Jones carry a wheelchair into the house?"

"Yes, sir. Like I said, he might have someone else in his sights."

"A dreadful thought, but I suppose it is possible." Matt rubbed his eyes as his brain churned busily.

"We should go and knock on the door," Dilys said. "There are four of us, plus the backup, and only two of them."

"As far as we know," Matt pointed out.

"Okay, but we have surprise on our side and what can they realistically do? It isn't as if the victims were shot to death. There's no indication that either man might have a gun. Move the backup a little closer, then we'll knock on the door and see what happens."

Matt almost laughed. "We need a better plan than 'see what happens'."

He stared at the house trying to work out what to do, when suddenly the front door opened. Gwyn Jones appeared on the step dressed in a dark overcoat and approached the car on the drive. Matt made a sudden decision.

"Dilys, with me. You two, get around to the back of the place and do it quietly. Do *not* announce our presence. Tell the rest of the team what's going on and that they are still on stand-by."

Matt walked quickly across the street and towards the house, Dilys with him. Gwyn Jones didn't spot them until the last moment when he turned towards the road.

"Is that Matt Lambert?" he asked, peering down the drive. "It is, isn't it? What a coincidence, I was chatting to Fabia recently. She came to visit and brought your little one with her. I must say, you have a beautiful daughter, obviously takes after her mother." He laughed. "What are you doing here?"

"We were out this way following a lead and I remembered Fabia said you lived here. I thought we'd beg a cuppa and ask if you have any thoughts about the murder case we're working on, bearing in mind you crossed swords with Jake Seddon in the past."

"I was just on my way out, but as it is important I'm happy to put the kettle on."

"Great, thanks."

Matt and Dilys followed Gwyn into the house and walked past a folded wheelchair in the hall, which they spotted simultaneously. A door off the hall, presumably the living room, was firmly shut so they followed Gwyn to the kitchen where he made tea.

Matt asked a few questions about Seddon, then suddenly changed direction. "Do you know a guy called Keith Prendergast? He's a freelance writer."

"Why are you asking about him?" Gwyn said.

"His name came up a couple of times in the investigation."

"In what respect?" Gwyn smiled. "If you give me a clue, I might be more helpful."

"I noticed a wheelchair in the hall, sir," Dilys said. "You don't look as though you need one and Fabia said you live alone."

Gwyn's face darkened. "Oh, now I see what this is all about. Your sudden interest in me was in fact you lot checking me out." He frowned. "You even sent your partner to do your dirty work for you. You must think I had something to do with those murders. Are you mad? What's my motive? Bitter retired cop, tortured by the 'ones who got away' and turning vigilante? Really?" Gwyn threw his head back and laughed before fixing Matt in his gaze. He took a breath. "I have to say, you've got a nerve coming to my house like this. How many plods did you bring with you?"

The kitchen door suddenly swung open and Keith Prendergast stood in the doorway. "What's going on, Gwyn?" He glared at the officers. "Why are you here?"

Matt got to his feet. "To arrest you and Gwyn Jones in connection with three murders."

Keith took a step back and held up his hands in a submissive gesture. "Hang on, mate," he said, "you've got this all wrong."

"I don't think so, and I am not your mate. If you are innocent, you'll have no problem explaining it all at the station."

"No, really, you're making a big mistake. We're on your side, so before you do anything hasty, come and meet the others."

Matt blinked and suddenly the ground beneath his feet didn't feel so solid. "Others?" he muttered.

Keeping a careful eye on both men, he allowed them to lead him and Dilys back along the hall and into a large room. As Matt stepped inside, he felt his stomach drop. Two women were sitting on easy chairs and looked up as the door opened. One was middle-aged, the other appeared to be approaching her nineties. Next to her chair, within easy reach, was a walking frame. She smiled at Matt.

"Hallo," she said. "Have you come to join our little club?"

"What club is that, madam?" he asked and felt a trickle of sweat run down his spine.

"Our murder club." The woman giggled. "Don't worry, we don't kill people – or each other. I'm a retired judge for goodness sake." She chuckled again. "No, what we do is try to solve crimes the police haven't been able to. Cold cases mainly, sometimes current. We are currently investigating a triple murder, very complex. That would be something to get your teeth into, eh? Start with a bang."

Matt blinked, not sure what to say. He could not believe he had got things so very wrong and wondered what Erica Talbot would say when he reported what had happened in the Mumbles. Dilys rescued him.

"Thanks very much," she said, "but we're not potential members, just checking in on Gwyn. DCI Lambert used to work with him and as we were passing…"

"Now that's a shame," the old lady said. "Our little band of sleuths achieves some good results and we're always interested in new members – especially police officers. The work is fascinating and Gwyn is a generous host." She grinned at the retired sergeant and sent him a saucy wink.

"It's a kind and tempting offer and we'll keep it in mind, but sadly we don't have enough time today. Enjoy your meeting and keep on catching bad guys."

Matt and Dilys backed out of the room. Gwyn and Keith were waiting in the hall with large, fairly unfriendly grins on their faces.

"I reckon you owe us an apology, boy," Gwyn said. "A bloody enormous one, although why you even thought I was involved is beyond me. Is the pressure of the job getting to you? Gets us all in the end."

"I'm sorry," Matt said. "When I heard how closely Mr Prendergast was following the investigation, then the wheelchair in the hall–"

"The wheelchair belongs to the judge," Gwyn said. "Why are you interested in it? Is a chair involved in your investigation? You should share, after all you owe me."

Matt shook his head. "I apologise again, but, Mr Prendergast, I do have to ask you where you were last Thursday from about five o'clock."

Gwyn and Keith looked at each other and laughed.

"Thursday?" Keith asked. "Bloody Thursday? We have our murder club on Thursdays don't we?"

"What other day of the week would we have it?" Gwyn asked with a grin. "Keith was with us all afternoon and evening. Until about seven, I'd say."

Keith nodded sternly.

Matt grimaced and tried to ignore the flush that was creeping up his neck. "My apologies again," he said. "I jumped to conclusions and should not have done so."

"Yes you did," Keith said, "the wrong conclusions."

Dilys passed Keith one of her cards. "Once again, we are very sorry to have disturbed you," she said. "If you do stumble upon anything useful, please do let us know."

Dilys headed for the front door, Matt right behind her. A spot was itching between his shoulder blades and he knew the men were still sending him evils. Once in the car, they ordered the backup home and recalled Sara and Craig. Matt then took a deep breath, rang Erica Talbot and confessed to her what had happened.

"Shit!" she said. "That's a fairly large cock-up, isn't it?"

"Yes, ma'am. I was so certain–"

"I'm sure there will be no lasting harm done. Everyone makes a mistake now and again, and when you told me what you had, I went along with your decision." She chuckled softly. "Perhaps Gwyn's little group would appreciate a visit from a high-ranking officer who has taken an interest. I'll smooth things over. For now though, get yourself back to the office and we'll talk again about Paul Michaelson."

"Yes, ma'am. I'll be there within the hour."

Matt disconnected the call. "Bloody hell, Dilys," he said. "This is a disaster."

"Not quite, sir, but close. The guv always has your back though, you know she does. Anyway, it could have been Gwyn for many reasons."

Matt shook his head. "No, it couldn't have been. Fabia told me it wasn't him and I should have listened to her. I'll be eating humble pie for weeks because of this."

"It might not be as bad as you think."

"It'll probably be a lot worse." He groaned loudly. "Right, get us back to base. I'll take my roasting from the guv, then we'll plan Michaelson's arrest." He groaned again and rubbed his eyes. "I should have taken a moment to think things through…"

## Chapter 27

The next morning, the sun was just beginning its slow crawl into a perfectly blue, spring sky as Matt assembled his team in the car park at the rear of the police station. Following the disaster of the day before, Erica Talbot had taken the decision that the youngest Michaelson should be arrested without delay, and a raid had been quickly planned. Matt wasn't expecting the arrest to be difficult, but no one could ever be sure how a suspect would react so backup was always the best idea. In one of the cars was an MOE – method of entry – team, complete with the equipment to smash through doors, but Matt hoped they wouldn't be necessary. He had already ensured that all officers would be wearing stab vests and was confident they all knew what they were doing, and what was expected. Following a few hurried last words, he signalled for the off. The drivers started the engines and followed Matt and Dilys as they pulled onto the main road and headed for the block of flats where their quarry lived.

Matt and Dilys travelled in silence, there was nothing left to say and both concentrated on the job in hand, hoping the next hour would go well and that there would be no mistakes or injuries. The vehicles reassembled in the road outside the block they were to target. Again, Matt took the lead and marched up to the front door of the Michaelsons' abode with Dilys a couple of steps behind.

He hammered on the door. "Police!" he shouted. "Open the door right now!"

He heard no movement from inside and hammered again. He tensed as he spotted a shadow approach the door and as soon as it was opened, he barged his way in with Dilys on his heels, four uniformed officers bringing up the rear.

"Hey," Paul protested. "What's going on?"

"Paul Michaelson, I am arresting you on suspicion of murder. You do not have to say anything, but it may harm your defence if you do not mention when questioned something which you later rely on in court. Anything you do say may be given in evidence. Get dressed, boy, you're coming with us."

"What? No! I'm not going anywhere with you. I haven't killed anyone."

Cari suddenly appeared in the narrow hallway, took one look at what was going on and wedged herself between Matt and her son.

"Leave him alone," she screamed. "He hasn't done anything and I won't let you take him."

"You must stand back," Matt warned her. "We have a warrant for his arrest and we *are* taking him in."

"No," Cari wailed. "You can't. You already have his brother and I can't lose my youngest as well. You're making a big mistake."

"Then we will discover the truth during interview and, if what you say is correct, he will be released. Now, move back." Matt turned and addressed the team. "Constable Evans, get Paul to put some trousers on and escort him to the car. The rest of you search his room and recover all digital equipment – you know the drill – together with anything else you find that might have a connection to our investigation."

The team began to carry out their orders as Dilys took hold of Cari's arm and encouraged her out of the way and into the living room.

"This is all wrong," Cari protested. "Paul hasn't done anything. He's a pussycat compared to Dai and you already have him locked up."

"As the chief inspector says, if we can satisfy ourselves he doesn't have anything to do with the murders as you believe, we will release him."

"I want to go with him. He's not good with people and you'll twist what he says, I know you will. It's happened before."

"That won't be possible. Paul is an adult, but he can have a solicitor with him."

"But I'm the one who knows him the best. He has mental health problems."

"The station doctor will check him over to make sure he's fit to be interviewed. You shouldn't worry too much, we will look after him."

"Like I trust you lot." Cari glanced up as Paul – now in handcuffs – was led past the living room door and leapt to her feet. Dilys grabbed her arm.

"Don't," Dilys warned. "If you cause a row, you'll be arrested too, then you really won't be able to help him. Let us do our job."

Cari shook her head in defeat and collapsed back on the sofa. Dilys was surprised to see tears on the woman's cheeks.

"You don't understand," she sobbed. "He's my carer. I need him and can't manage here on my own."

"Maybe your mother will sit with you," Dilys suggested. "She lives a block or two over, doesn't she? I could have someone fetch her if you like."

"I don't want her here, she's old and not useful for anything much. Anyway, this business would upset her."

"Well, if you're sure."

"I am. Just get this over with as quickly as possible, then get out of my flat."

* * *

By the time Matt and Dilys arrived at the station, Paul Michaelson had been processed by the custody officer and was safely locked in a cell.

"Let's grab a cuppa, Dilys," Matt said. "We deserve a breather and there's no rush. The duty solicitor is still on his way." They walked upstairs to the squad room and Matt smiled. "That all went like clockwork this morning. I wish every arrest was as straightforward, although, I did wonder whether Cari would kick off." He poured two mugs of coffee from the glass jug in the kitchen area.

"Me too, actually," Dilys said. "Proper tamping, she was, but upset as well. I know she's not the nicest of people, but she hates the idea of losing a second son to the system. Such different and difficult lives people have. When I left her on the sofa, she looked… bereft, lost and lonely."

"Sounds as though you feel sorry for her."

"I do a bit, after all it is her sons who break the law. No evidence that she ever has."

"Fair point. Maybe I'll have Chloe pop round to check on her."

"Good idea, sir."

"Okay then, let's get on. Round up all the files and reports. I want as much to hand as possible to throw at him."

A nearby phone rang and Matt answered it. He listened for a moment, muttered his thanks and hung up. "The duty solicitor's turned up. Seems he doesn't want to talk to his client before we start, so we can go on down."

"Rightio, sir."

* * *

Matt and Dilys settled at the table in the dreary interview room with a picture of the Newport Wave on the wall. A few moments later, Paul Michaelson slouched in with a uniformed officer and flopped on the empty chair without catching anyone's eye. Dilys started the recording equipment, verbally logged the date, time and those in the room, then reminded Paul he was being interviewed under caution. She also told him that if he wanted to speak confidentially to his solicitor, the officers would leave the room.

"Do you understand what I've told you, Paul?" she asked.

He gave a small nod.

"You'll have to speak for the tape."

"Yes then, I get it."

"Do you understand why you are here?"

"Because you lot dragged me out of the flat not long after it was light."

"You're here," Dilys explained, "because we've arrested you on suspicion of involvement with the deaths of these men." She spread the photos on the table.

Paul and his solicitor leaned closer to look at them. Paul grinned.

"Well, that's alright then, innit? I haven't had anything to do with people dying, see? I've never killed anyone and bet you a tenner I'll walk out of here. You can't have any evidence that I've murdered anyone because I haven't."

He leaned back in his chair and tried to look relaxed and almost pulled it off. Matt couldn't tell whether the prisoner was telling the truth or was just a good actor. He didn't seem concerned enough about the position he was in and Matt decided he needed to change that.

"We went to see Dai yesterday," he said. "He sends his love to you and your mam. We wondered if he'd been giving you orders about how to keep the business running, but he denied this. He said you were working on your own initiative. He sounded proud, to be honest with you."

Paul grinned. "He's right. No one tells me what to do."

"So, what you have been doing?"

"Oh, a bit of this and that. Cash-in-hand jobs sometimes. Nothing illegal though. Nothing like murder."

"Dai told us you have been renting out the warehouse he owns. He told us he was surprised that none of the rent money had made it into his prison account." Matt smiled across the table. "Who did you rent to, Paul?"

The prisoner's shoulders slumped lower. He kept his eyes on the tabletop and shook his head. Matt slid the photos of Geddings and Seddon closer. He saw Paul's eyes widen in recognition.

"We know these two men were tenants of yours. We can prove it too. DNA, fingerprints, all the clever stuff. Where did you kill them? We know it wasn't in the same place you tortured others who hadn't paid their dues."

Paul shook his head again. "Tortured? Really? This is a bloody fairy tale and you know it. I *didn't* kill them."

Matt put Prosser's photo on top of the others. "This is another of your victims. Tell us how you knew him."

"I didn't."

"And I don't believe you."

Paul shrugged. "I don't care what you think or believe. I didn't do it, and because I didn't, you won't find any evidence saying I did. So, me? I'm not bothered."

Matt opened the thick file and flipped sheets before looking back across the table at Paul. "We've been monitoring your internet use and your mobile phone. What we have discovered leads us to believe that you are dealing. You've got a little gang of runners, haven't you? We're not sure what it is you're selling yet but trust me, we will find out."

"Dai told us he had heard you were selling smuggled tobacco," Dilys said.

Paul's face relaxed a little. "Yeah, that's what I've been doing, just a few pouches a week, nothing big. So nick me for that and I'll confess if you want."

Paul grinned and his solicitor placed a warning hand on his client's arm.

"I think a short chat with my client would be beneficial," the man said.

"Of course," Matt said and got to his feet. "We'll grab a cuppa. Would you or your client like something to drink?"

"No, thanks, we're fine."

Dilys leaned across the table to switch off the recorder. "Interview suspended at 10.45." She got to her feet and followed Matt out of the room.

Erica Talbot was waiting for them at the reception area of the custody suite.

"How is it going?' she asked.

Matt groaned. "Slowly, I think describes it. The interview feels like the case, lots of little bits of information or evidence that don't fit neatly together. Early days though."

"Do you have a view on whether he is guilty?'

"He's the logical suspect. He had the means and the methods. He was in the right place and he could have broken fingers like his big brother…" Matt grimaced. "Yes, it could have been Paul, but he insists it wasn't. He never blinks when we push."

"Psychopathic tendencies maybe?"

"His mam told me he had mental health issues," Dilys said.

"I'll speak to his doctor," Erica said. "We have plenty of time so we'll find out what we're dealing with before you tackle him again. We may need someone from the mental health team to attend." She turned away then looked back. "Go and get some lunch, the pair of you, while I sort this out. You did well this morning. A good clean arrest that won't make the front page in the morning."

* * *

Fabia heard a car pull up outside the house and looked out of the front window. She was delighted to see Matt getting out of the passenger seat. Leaving Bethan in her playpen, she went to the hall and opened the front door.

"I wasn't expecting to see you before supper time," she said. "Dilys too. Are you playing truant?"

Matt chuckled. "No, actually, we're following orders. Erica told us to get some lunch and I thought…"

"That I'd have enough food in the fridge to feed two hungry coppers."

"Something like that," Matt admitted then looked concerned. "Have you?"

"I'm sure I can rustle something up."

Fabia followed them to the kitchen and put on a pot of coffee. "I take it the arrest went well? Or maybe he got away and you're hiding here from Erica."

Matt snatched her arm and kissed her. "It went perfectly."

"Then, sit down and tell me while I make some" – she peered into the fridge – "cheesy scrambled eggs and tomatoes on toast." She backed out and waved a packet in the air. "I've even got some bacon."

"Perfect, thank you, my lovely."

"Less flattery, more debrief. I want all the details."

Matt's story ended as they finished their meal. He drained his coffee and poured another mug. "Gosh this is so much better than anything at the station."

"I should hope so," Fabia huffed. She collected the plates. "Do you think Paul is guilty?" she asked.

Matt sighed deeply. "I think this is the first suspect I've interviewed that I don't lean one way or the other. He's a bit stroppy but I can't say he's lying. He freely admitted to selling baccy but nothing more, and continues to deny he killed or tortured anyone without so much as a twitch."

"So if not Paul, who else would do that?"

"I honestly don't know. Some of the people we've spoken to during the investigation are angry enough to kill one of the men, but not all of them. Paul is definitely connected to the first two victims. He hasn't admitted that yet, but when we receive the all-clear we'll have another go. Maybe by then his solicitor will have given him some good advice."

Dilys got to her feet and walked over to the sink. "That brunch was fabulous, Fabia, I'll just get the washing up done."

"There's no need."

Dilys shook her head and began loading plates into the sink and filling it with hot water. She glanced towards the playpen and waved at Bethan, who grabbed her toes and giggled.

"She's a little smasher isn't she? Such a happy little soul."

"I'm not going to disagree," Fabia said. "Her first teeth are coming through and she doesn't like that, but she's easy to distract." She looked at Matt. "Will you interview Paul again this afternoon?"

"That's the plan if he passes the medical exam."

"Do you think he is mentally ill?"

"Personally, I don't, but I'm not an expert. His mother told Dilys he is, which was why we were granted a lunch break." He looked at his watch. "Actually we ought to get back. There's more to do apart from the interview." He got to his feet, bent into the playpen to tickle his daughter, then shrugged into his jacket. He gave Fabia a quick hug and a peck on the cheek. "Thank you for feeding us. That was a lovely meal."

"My pleasure. Any idea what time you might be home?"

"None at all, I'm afraid, but we're on the home run now, I'm sure we are. No more late nights when this is over."

Fabia smiled. "Until the next case."

# Chapter 28

Matt and Dilys had only been in the interview room with Paul and his solicitor for half an hour, when there was a soft tap on the door. Matt frowned, irritated by the interruption, and glanced over his shoulder. The door cracked open and Chloe looked in.

"I'm sorry, sir," she said. "I have something to show you."

"Can't it wait?" he asked.

"No, sir, I don't think it can."

After a moment's hesitation, Matt got to his feet and excused himself from the interview, closing the door behind him.

"What is it, Chloe?" he asked.

"I went to see Cari, to check on her as you said. Anyway, she was a mess, looked like she'd been crying ever since you arrested her boy. I made her a cup of tea, had a chat, like, and after a while she told me to go. Said she'd be okay, but I wasn't so sure."

"Chloe," Matt said, "I'm in the middle of an interview. Tell me what's important."

"Yes, sir, sorry. When I left, I decided to visit her mother. I thought that perhaps she could keep an eye on

Cari, give her a ring or something. Anyway, I found her place, a ground floor flat in the next block over, and got invited in for a cuppa."

"And?"

Chloe switched on her mobile phone, tapped and swiped at the screen then handed the device to her boss. "You need to come with me to see this for yourself, sir, before speaking to Paul again. Dilys too."

Matt nodded as he peered at the image on the small screen. "Yes, you're right. We'll put this on hold and see you upstairs. Good work, Chloe."

Matt ducked back into the interview room and announced his presence for the tape. "I am suspending the interview," he said. "Something has come up and I need to be somewhere else." He turned to the duty solicitor. "I'll make sure Paul is given a meal and you are welcome to spend more time with him. Interview suspended at 16.34." Matt snapped off the machine and glanced at Dilys. "I need you with me, Sergeant," he said and left the room.

* * *

Chloe was waiting for them with a car and as she drove to the estate, Matt told Dilys where they were heading. Chloe parked close to the block and together they walked to the ground floor flat she indicated.

"Does the old lady know we are coming?" Dilys asked.

"I did say I'd be popping back, but not why," Chloe said. "I also gave Karen Johns from SOCO a ring and she's on her way over."

"Good idea," Matt said as he knocked on the door.

A very short, hunched-over woman, with wild grey hair opened it and peered out carefully. "Oh," she said. "I didn't think you'd be back so soon. Got company too, I see."

"These are my bosses, Chief Inspector Lambert, and Sergeant Bevan. Can we come in for a word?"

"Is my daughter alright?" the woman asked. "I gave her a ring after you'd left, but all she does is cry. Couldn't get any sense out of her and it's not so easy for me to get to her. Has something bad happened?"

"As far as we know, she is okay," Matt said.

The woman nodded and stood back from the door. "Come in then, keep the cold out."

Matt squeezed past her, walked along the hall and stopped when he reached the kitchen. He looked into the room and was aware of a smile blossoming on his face.

"You use a wheelchair, madam?" he asked.

"Yes, have done a few years now. Bad arthritis and a dodgy hip on one side. I can just about manage indoors, but can't walk any distance really. My grandson is very good at taking me shopping once a week and it's nice to get out every so often, rather than being stuck in here for days on end."

A knock on the door announced Karen's presence and Chloe went to let her in.

"Does your grandson ever borrow your chair?" Dilys asked.

"Occasionally, but not very often, only really to bring stuff from the market, if he has to pick up a bag of spuds or anything heavy. Easier to wheel it home than carry it."

Karen examined the chair paying particular attention to the tyre on one side. After a few minutes, she straightened up and nodded at Matt.

"I'm sorry, madam," she said, "but we need to borrow your chair for a while."

"You can't take my wheelchair. How can I get around without it?" She looked suspicious. "Why do you want it?"

"I'm sure we can arrange a replacement and you will get yours back as soon as we've been able to take a look at it."

"You can look at it here, surely."

"We need a closer look, there are some tests we need to run."

"Oh, I don't understand any of this, really I don't. It can't be right taking an old woman's wheelchair away."

Karen slipped her phone from her pocket. "I'll ring the local health board to arrange for them to bring you a loan chair and I'll make sure they know it is urgent."

"Doesn't sound like I have much say in the matter," the woman grumbled. "As long as I have another one, I guess I'll manage, but I want mine back as soon as possible."

"We will certainly be as quick as we can."

Matt watched as Karen placed plastic bags over the handles, a protective cover on the seat and back, and a larger, bin-sized bag over the entire chair before sealing it with tape. With help from Chloe, she lifted it up and carried it from the flat. They loaded the chair into the SOCO van and Karen smiled at Matt.

"Looks to me as though you've had a lucky break, sir," she said.

"Not me, Chloe found it, but yes, a huge stroke of luck. How long will you need before you can confirm this was used to move the bodies?"

"Shouldn't be too long. At first look the scuffed tyre matches the impressions collected at the body dumps, and I'm fairly sure there are a couple of small patches of blood on the seat, another on the backrest. I'll get this to base and begin work immediately, take samples of the blood, mud trapped in the treads on the tyres, and fingerprints, of course. I'll put a rush on any DNA tests required and will try to get back to you later today. If that's not possible, first thing tomorrow."

"Marvellous. Do your best."

"Always." Karen nodded. She got into the van, started the engine and pulled away.

Matt returned to the flat, told the elderly lady what was happening and that a replacement chair should be delivered within the hour, then went out to the car with Dilys and Chloe and headed back to the station.

"It looks as though we have him, sir," Dilys said from the back seat. "That was the break we needed. Well done, Chloe."

The younger officer concentrated on the road, but a huge smile creased her face. "Just doing my job," she muttered proudly.

* * *

Back at the station, Matt ran upstairs to tell Erica the good news. She was suitably delighted and arranged for her secretary to bring in a celebratory coffee and a plate of biscuits.

"I knew you'd get there in the end," she said. "Karen was *sure* the wheelchair you recovered was the one that left the impressions at the body dumps?"

"As sure as she can be with such a quick look, but she will be running tests. With a bit of luck, she'll come back to me this evening."

"At least you have some hard evidence to put to the suspect now. Will you mention it when you resume the interview?"

"Yes, I intend to. Maybe his mask will slip when he knows we have the chair." Matt sipped from his cup. "We might even be able to get a confession from him. If we fail, I am conscious that the clock is ticking and am minded to charge him. We have enough, I'm sure we do. We can take him to court in the morning and have him remanded, which will buy us some time for the rest of the results to come in." Matt put his cup back on the tray. "We still haven't been able to prove a link between him and Prosser though, and I must admit that does bother me. A loose end I can't tie up."

"You'll get there, I'm sure, and as you say, you'll have much more time once Michaelson is tucked up in Newport remand centre. Well done, Matt. A great piece of work. Keep me informed on any developments, will you? I'm looking forward to announcing to the press that we have charged someone and wipe those self-satisfied smiles from their faces."

Matt got to his feet and smiled at his boss. "Of course we'll keep you in the loop, ma'am."

He turned on his heel, left the office and ran downstairs to congratulate his team and give Paul the good news – that he was going to be charged with the murder of three men.

* * *

Back in the interview room, Matt took a deep breath and looked across the table at Paul. He knew this would be the final round before the lad was charged and the more evidence Matt could glean now, the easier it would be to convince the CPS he had a case. He smiled at the prisoner who smiled back as though he was in a café, not an interview room. Dilys set up the recording equipment, and stated the date, time and the names of those in the room. She also stated the recording was the resumption of a previous interview.

Matt didn't speak for several moments. He flipped through some pages in a cardboard folder, before removing one and placing it on the table in front of Paul.

"What's that?" Paul asked.

"You don't recognise where the picture was taken?" Matt asked.

Paul said nothing.

"It was taken in your nan's kitchen, and that's her wheelchair next to the door."

"So?"

"Your DNA is all over that chair."

"Again – so? I take her out in it."

"Where do you take her?" Dilys asked.

"To the shops mainly, supermarket up the hill, sometimes to the pond in the park, to her mate's houses. Anywhere she wants, really. Why are you interested in her chair? She's old and can't walk. End of."

"We think you borrowed her chair to move the men you killed." Matt fixed Paul in his gaze, but Paul didn't look away.

"What the…?" Paul laughed suddenly. "What a wind up! From start to finish you've been winding me up." He glanced at his solicitor. "Can't you get me out of here? They shouldn't be allowed to spout rubbish like that with no evidence of anything. Dead bodies in wheelchairs?" He laughed again. "I can't wait to tell my nan, she'll wet her pants."

The solicitor looked at Matt. "Can you link the chair to the locations where the bodies were found?"

"The chair is with forensics for further tests, but yes, we believe we can."

"What is your next move?"

"I intend to charge your client, hold him overnight, and take him to court in the morning. We will of course oppose any application for bail."

"No, you can't!" Paul yelled. "You can't do this. I have to look after Mam and Gran. Honestly, I didn't kill those men, really I didn't. I've never broken anyone's fingers or tortured anyone either. I don't understand why you don't believe me."

"We have evidence to prove what you did. Why don't you tell us what really happened?"

"Because you don't listen and won't believe anything I say… and my solicitor says I talk too much." Paul scrubbed at his face.

"We have reason to believe that you tortured and murdered three men in cold blood and used your grandmother's wheelchair to dump their bodies in locations around the Pontygwyn area. Why did you do it, Paul? We know your links with Geddings and Seddon. How did you know Huw Prosser?"

Paul shook his head and stared at the floor until a uniformed officer came to take him to be charged. Matt leaned back in his chair and yawned as Dilys turned off the recorder, removed the discs and labelled them carefully, as the solicitor left the room.

"That was a busy day," Matt said. "Worth it, though. Suspect charged and court in the morning. Are you going to attend?"

"Of course," Dilys said. "I was rather hoping I'd be part of the escort. I like to see a case through."

Matt smiled. "I'll see what I can do. You should get off now though, it's late. Tomorrow will be another busy day, hopefully the results will begin flooding in and we need to start building the case – but not tonight." He got to his feet. "I'm knocking off too, so I'll see you here at eight tomorrow. Today was a good day, Dilys, a very good day."

"Yes, sir. Have a nice evening, what's left of it."

* * *

After Dilys had left, Matt sent Fabia a text telling her he was on his way, then went out to the car and drove to Pontygwyn. When he pulled up in the drive, Fabia opened the door and spilt light from the hall into the darkness. Matt locked the car, walked over to her and held her tightly. She returned his embrace and they stayed that way for some moments.

"Let's get in," she said eventually. "I can see how tired you are. Have you eaten?"

"One of the lads went out for burgers and pizzas," Matt confessed, "so I've been fed."

"Go to the living room then and I'll fetch us something to drink. Bethan is already in bed so we can have a little spell of quiet time. You look like you can do with some of that."

"Sounds exactly what I need."

"Sit by the fire. I'll be there in a minute and you can tell me what's happened."

He did as she suggested and flopped on the easy chair positioned on one side of the fire. He loosened his tie, kicked off his shoes and stretched his feet towards the grate. Fabia joined him a couple of minutes later and chuckled.

"Didn't take you long to look as though you've been here all night."

"Wish I had."

"Here's the deal. I'll keep the glasses topped up for as long as you talk."

"Sounds fair."

Fabia sat in the opposite chair and stirred the embers with a long brass poker as Matt told her about the arrest, the interviews, and the discovery of the wheelchair. He told her that Paul had been charged and would appear in court in the morning, and that Erica Talbot would be speaking to the press.

"It was a strange case," he said. "Everything fit and nothing fit. Didn't seem to quite come together. I'm hoping Karen will have something for us in the morning that might clear things up." He yawned.

"I suppose you are expecting to find matches to the three victims?"

Matt smiled. "That would certainly be brilliant if it is as simple as that, but whatever is? My problem is Prosser. I can't get that man out of my head. I still don't know where he came from, and still can't prove that he had ever met Paul Michaelson. It just doesn't quite fit and it's really irritating me. Chloe thinks he's been hiding, or someone was hiding him…" Matt frowned. "Damn, I nearly had something then, but it's gone."

"If you try to forget about it now, it might come to you tomorrow. I get thoughts like that all the time and eventually they come through." Fabia chuckled. "It's all well and good being able to remember things, but finding them again in my internal filing cabinets can sometimes be more difficult than I like."

Matt laughed and topped up their glasses. "I'd better make this the last," he said, "as pleasant as this is, I'm taking Paul to court in the morning. Need to be in at eight to organise it."

"That's okay, we can stay up late and drink too much tomorrow when your prisoner is locked up. You're surely due a couple of days off."

"Yeah, maybe. Let's see how it goes in the morning. Have you got plans for tomorrow?"

"Not really, another meeting of the LSBC has been cancelled… well, postponed." She sighed. "Too many of the members don't seem to want to take this seriously enough and use any excuse to delay meetings. I'm actually getting a bit fed up with it to be honest, but didn't want to say anything because Erica Talbot worked so hard to get me the post."

"I'm sure she won't mind if you speak to her. She's very keen on communication with those working with her, and she listens. In fact…"

"What?"

"She was talking the other day about you maybe coming back on her team. That's where she really wants you, I reckon."

"You're kidding."

"No, Fabia, I'm not."

"Maybe I will give her ring then, but no, not many plans for tomorrow though. I've a couple of pen and ink drawings to finish, but the weather is going to be nice so there's always washing, and Cath rang earlier. She has returned from her sister's house and says she'll pop in for coffee. She sounded much happier than when she left."

"That sounds like a pretty full-on day to me." Matt yawned again and apologised.

"No need, my love. You're up early tomorrow, so we'll call it a night. Look in on Bethan for me, but don't wake her."

"I'll try very hard not to," Matt said and got to his feet. "Don't be long, *cariad*."

# Chapter 29

Matt and Dilys shared an early coffee in his office and checked through the paperwork needed for the court. While Dilys immersed herself in the digital file, Matt searched through a pile of internal post.

"Ha!" he said suddenly, making Dilys jump. "This is what I was waiting for." He tore open the flap and began to skim-read the contents, verbalizing key points in an odd, disjointed fashion.

"Scuffed tyre… exact match… mud in treads… blood on chair… DNA…" There was a longer pause then he looked up at Dilys and smiled. "The DNA matches all three victims and the wheelchair *was* at the body dumps. That's what I call a slam dunk. Bloody marvellous!"

"No chance of bail for Michaelson then," Dilys said. "Will you tell him what we have before he steps into court?"

"No, it wouldn't add anything to the proceedings this morning and we need some more time to assess the new evidence. However, in the spirit of full disclosure I'll give the duty solicitor a quick call. He might be able to get Paul to change his plea, which would save time."

"Yes, maybe. Can I take a look?"

Matt handed the report to Dilys who frowned as she read through the results. After a while, she looked up. "Did you see Karen identified a hair recovered from the back of the seat as belonging to Prosser?"

"I did and it proves he was transported in the chair, but it still doesn't tell us who Prosser actually was. Everyone comes from somewhere, but not him it seems."

"His lack of background bothered me too. I didn't think I'd ever known anyone without some sort of history, but then I realised I did. One of my first jobs was guarding a woman in a flat in Cardiff, in witness protection."

"And you think Prosser was in a similar position? What could he have witnessed?"

"I don't know, sir, but I'd like to take a dig around to satisfy myself."

"I'm not sure how likely that scenario is, but yes of course you're welcome to make other enquiries." He looked up at the clock above the door. "We had better crack on and deliver Michaelson to court. When he's been remanded and is on his way, there's a place around the corner from the court that cooks a great all-day breakfast. My treat."

* * *

At around the time that Paul Michaelson was being locked in a holding cell after being remanded, Fabia opened the back door of the kitchen and allowed a shaft of sunshine inside. She took a deep breath of the spring air and decided it was warm enough to take Bethan into the garden. She gathered a thick rug with a waterproof backing and added Bethan's favourite teddy to the top of the laundry basket. Then, with her daughter on one hip, the basket of washing on the other, she went out to the garden. She made sure Bethan was settled, then carried the washing to the line and began to peg it out. She heard the click of the side gate and turned expecting to see Cath, but was surprised to see a stocky woman, with short black hair and a pinched face, wearing a pink tracksuit complete with hood, walking across the lawn towards her.

"Hallo," Fabia said. "Can I help you?" Fabia searched her memory. She knew she had seen the woman before but couldn't recall where or when.

The woman smiled and kept walking. "You might be able to," she said. "I'm looking for a policeman, Chief Inspector Lambert. Someone down the road says he lives here."

Bethan giggled loudly and threw her teddy onto the grass.

The woman looked down. "Oh, what a little sweetie. Is she yours?"

"She is, yes. Can you tell me what you want with Matt? I might be able to help you."

"Just a quick word, bit of advice that's all. I take it you're his partner. Bit older than him, aren't you? Not what I was expecting." She took another couple of steps closer to the rug and dropped to her knees. "Look at you, my sweetheart. What a pretty little girl you are. I always wanted a girl but all God gave me was a pair of lumbering lummoxes. Took after their da, both of them." She laughed suddenly. "At least he's not around anymore."

Before Fabia really understood what had happened, the woman had gathered Bethan into her arms and was rocking her on her lap. Fabia blinked and with a jolt recognised Cari Michaelson.

"Cari," Fabia said, "please, put my daughter down."

"She's fine with me, aren't you, little darling." She held one of Bethan's tiny hands between her thumb and forefinger and rubbed gently. Bethan smiled and waved her free hand in the air.

"Tell me what you want," Fabia said, not taking her eyes off the pair.

"I already told you. A word with this little one's daddy. I want to talk to him about my youngest, Paul."

"You could have just rung him at the station."

"Yeah, I thought about it, but face to face is better. He needs to know what he's doing to my family. Paul is no killer, yet he's on his way to the remand centre. I need him at home with me, can't manage without him. He's my registered carer."

Without hesitation, Fabia decided to take a different path. She tried to recall what she had been taught about hostage negotiation during basic training, a lifetime ago.

"I didn't know that you are unwell, Cari. What's wrong?"

"Bad back, awful pain. Doctor says there's nothing he can do."

"I'm sorry. Paul helps you, does he?"

Bethan tugged at Cari's ear and she pulled a comical face.

"Yes, he's a good boy to his mother; not the fizziest pop in the fridge, but he does his best to take care of me. That's what I want to tell your boyfriend, and why he has to let him out. I went to court this morning and couldn't get my head round the fact he didn't get bail. He has responsibilities."

"That would have been taken into account," Fabia said, hoping to keep Cari's attention on her, while she tried to control the panic rising inside her. "Unfortunately, it doesn't mean much in a murder case. No one charged with murder would be granted bail."

Cari frowned. "That's not true, some do. Not the likes of us though, the cops have always had it in for us. No wonder my old man legged it, he should have taken us with him."

"How about I give Matt a ring, let him know you're here and would like to see him? Then we can go in and have a cuppa while we wait for him to arrive."

Cari seemed to think about it. She ruffled Bethan's curls then moved her own thumb and forefinger to the child's toes and tickled. Bethan giggled.

"Yeah, go on then, ring him, but we'll wait out here. Tell him to be quick."

"Can I take the baby from you?"

"No, I've told you we're fine – aren't we, my lovely? When you ring him tell him to come on his own, if I see anyone else with him, well…"

"Well what?"

Cari's face twisted into a cruel grin. "I can't imagine it would take much to break baby fingers, can you?"

Fabia took a step closer and Cari took hold of Bethan's hand. "Just make the call and keep away. I don't want to hurt her, but if your fella isn't here in ten minutes, I will. You can trust me on that."

* * *

Matt took the call just as he was about to put a forkful of food into his mouth. Dilys saw all the colour leave her boss's face and when he cut the call and leapt to his feet, she did the same.

"What's up?" she asked.

"Fabia needs me! Cari's turned up and has hold of Bethan. I've got ten minutes to get there."

"The car's outside, we'll blue light it."

They dashed from the café, scrabbled into the car and Dilys set off for Pontygwyn, sirens screaming. Matt felt a trickle of sweat running down his back as he clung to the grab rail, willing Dilys to drive even faster. After what seemed like an hour later, she skidded to a halt outside the house within the allotted time span and opened her door.

"No!" Matt said. "Stay here! Cari has threatened to hurt my baby if I arrive with anyone else."

"But–"

"Just wait!"

Matt left the car, ran to the side gate leading to the back garden and blasted through. The sight of Cari sitting on the rug, cuddling Bethan close, made him stop in his tracks. Fabia stood close by and glanced over her shoulder.

"Stay where you are," she ordered. "Cari wants to talk to you, but you mustn't come any closer."

He could see the fear flushing his partner's skin. He wanted nothing more than to punch Cari hard in the face and reclaim his child, but the fear he'd recognised in Fabia's eyes stopped him. He took a couple of steps closer.

"Cari," he said. "What are you doing? Why are you even here?"

"You need to release my boy," Cari said. "He hasn't done what you've accused him of, I know he hasn't and he shouldn't be locked up."

"How do you know he's innocent?" Matt asked.

Fabia took half a step forward and Cari glared at her.

"Don't move!" Cari warned. "Any closer and I'll start breaking fingers."

Fabia quivered, not with fear, but hot anger. In a situation like this, properly controlled anger was a useful ally. But she was too far away, so she took a deep breath and focused her entire attention on the woman holding her daughter.

"Not nice, is it?" Cari asked. "Doesn't feel good to have your child threatened, does it?"

"Tell me," Matt said as he tried to quell his worse fear, "how are you certain Paul is innocent?"

Cari smiled and looked up at him. "Because it was me. I killed those men, all three of them."

"You? Why did you do that?"

"I didn't like what they were doing, and them using my premises to do it, not that they paid the rent, either of them. They needed reminding." She smiled down at Bethan and played again with her tiny fingers. "Jake was responsible for the deaths of another woman's children, and Seth was terrorizing single women, stealing money from them and driving them to destruction."

She lifted Bethan high above her head and swung her from left to right and Fabia forgot to breathe. The little girl laughed, unaware of the danger she was in.

"What about Prosser?" Matt asked, anxious to keep her talking. "Why did you kill him?"

"He was bothering the vicar, Cath Temple. I like the vicar, she was good to me and Dai after he was sent down, visited both of us when no one else cared. When I heard he'd tried it on and smacked her… well, that was the final straw. I knew he wouldn't stop and had to be made to stop." She looked at Fabia. "Look at you, a quivering wreck, pathetic."

Fabia wiped her face, her brain unable to decide what action she should take. It was as though the grey matter had frozen like a computer screen. As she looked back up she thought she spotted a quick movement from the corner of the house. She kept her gaze fixed on Cari, not wanting the woman to look behind her. Cath suddenly appeared and moved along the back wall, keeping to the shadows. Fabia wondered if Matt had seen her too and hoped he wouldn't do anything to draw attention to her friend as she crept slowly past the house and along the lawn edging the flower beds, using the larger shrubs as cover.

"Please," Fabia said, "don't hurt Bethan. She's an innocent in all this. You've confessed now, so why not go to the station with Matt and make it official? Your son will be released so he can take care of your mother, and you'll get what you want."

Cari laughed nastily. "You think I want to spend twenty years in a prison cell? Not a chance. I'll just hold onto this little one until Paul is set free, then make sure your boyfriend does what's right and gives me a chance to get away and make a new start. I'm not a bad person. I'm just an ordinary woman trying to hold her family together, and those bastards deserved what they got."

Cath was closer now, moving incredibly slowly towards the woman on the rug. Suddenly, only a step away from Cari, Cath lifted her hands. Fabia spotted a flash of light as Cath swung an object through the air, bringing it down hard on the side of Cari's head. The woman howled like an injured animal. She let go of Bethan who tumbled to the rug and rolled away while Cari scrabbled at her injured head and face. Fabia took two huge strides and snatched her daughter into her arms. Matt appeared by her side, took hold of Cari, forced her arms behind her back and fastened them with a zip tie from his pocket. He pulled her upright and held a handkerchief to the side of her face to staunch the flow of blood.

"Dilys," he screamed loudly. "Call for an ambulance and backup, then get in here."

Cath stood close by, rooted to the spot, a long-handled trowel dangling from one hand. Fabia moved to stand next to her friend, wrapped her spare arm around her and discovered she was shaking violently.

"Hey," she said. "Everything's okay now. Come and sit on the bench with me." She smiled. "Maybe leave the trowel here."

Cath blinked and looked down at the elongated tool, blood on the blade, and allowed it to slip from her grasp. They moved slowly across the lawn together and perched on an old wooden bench which faced the Black Mountains.

"I don't know how to thank you," Fabia said and held Bethan tightly. "You were fantastic!"

Cath shook her head. "No, don't say that, look at what I've done."

"What you have done is save my daughter. You did something extraordinary today and I will never be able to repay you."

# Epilogue

Easter Sunday

Fabia was busy at the stove when the doorbell rang.

"Matt," she called. "Get the door, will you? I've got my hands full."

She heard him run down the stairs, open the front door and greet their guests. A few moments later, he ushered Erica Talbot and Cath Temple into the warm kitchen which was filled with the scent of roasting meat. He carried Bethan to the table and sat her in her high chair.

"Hallo, Fabia," Erica said. "Can I give you hand?"

"Thank you, but I wouldn't dream of it. I'm nearly done, which leaves you enough time to pour the wine."

Cath held up a couple of bottles. "My sister lives near a vineyard so I bought some samples back from my mini break."

Matt helped Fabia carry dishes to the table and carved thick slices of lamb. The group helped themselves to vegetables, and began the meal.

After a while, Erica said, "This is such a treat, Fabia, I really appreciate the invite."

"I'm very pleased you found the time to come. I've cooked for Cath every Easter Sunday I've known her and always prepare too much food. Anyway," she said with a smile, "we have something to celebrate. The successful conclusion to a very difficult and serious investigation that had such a perfect ending."

"Yes, indeed, a fine piece of work."

"With a hefty dollop of luck," Matt said. "When I saw Cari with Bethan in her arms, my blood ran cold." He shuddered visibly. "I felt powerless and have never experienced fear like it before."

Fabia patted his arm and he grasped her hand. "I know," she said. She looked over at Cath. "But we experienced our very own miracle in the guise of a fierce, avenging angel."

Cath blushed. "Don't be silly, Fabia. How much wine have you had?"

"I know what I saw. You saved our little girl and you were… magnificent."

"I only did what anyone would have done. I could see she was so focused on you and Matt while she made her confession, that I knew she wouldn't hear me coming. I didn't set out to hurt her, just take Bethan away, but the trowel was sticking out of the flower bed and I picked it up." Cath groaned and put her face in her hands. "I can't believe what I've done. Violence is never right, not in any circumstances. What will my congregation think of me?"

"That you're a hero," Erica said. "No charges will be brought as two very reliable witnesses have made statements that put you firmly in the clear. It is certainly not in the public interest to prosecute a local vicar who saved a child from potentially serious harm."

"Cari talked about you, Cath," Fabia said, "while we were waiting for Matt. She heard what Prosser had done to you and told us how good you had been to her and Dai after he was sent down. Visited them both regularly."

"Only what I'd do for any parishioner who requests a pastoral visit."

"She obviously got a taste for vigilantism," Matt said. "When Paul rented the warehouse to the other two, she stalked them online, discovered a lot she didn't like and decided to put things right. During the official interview she made a full confession." He sipped from his wine glass and shook his head. "I still can't believe how *cryf* she is. Built like a bloody ox! All that nonsense about having a bad back and needing care when all the while she was carrying dead bodies around."

"Did she tell you what all the scratches were about?" asked Fabia.

"She said she just wanted to give them a good scare to teach them a lesson," Matt said. "The scratches were never supposed to be words or letters at all. And the London cab turned out to be just a big black people carrier that her mother has access to through a local mobility scheme. She gave us the location of where she'd killed them too; another warehouse linked to some bloke who's been inside for the last ten years. We'll have to run some tests on it to check for DNA but there's no real need for that. As you know, she entered a guilty plea and as she was remanded to await sentencing, she looked at me and said, 'I need a rest.'"

"Let's hope it's a very long one." Erica raised a glass. "A toast, to brave friends."

The group lingered over the meal and then shared a brandy with coffee.

"I have a little more news," Erica said. "Dilys Evans was right on the money about Huw Prosser." She sipped from her glass. "I got a call from my opposite number in North Norfolk and had an interesting conversation. He said our searches had alerted the witness protection people and he wanted to see if he could help out and give us a bit of background. He knew Huw Prosser – or Hilary Parker as he was originally named – from a case over there."

"What kind of case was it?"

"Prosser worked as an accountant for a very large, very dodgy waste disposal company. The owners of the company were connected to organised crime and had been under investigation for quite some time. Prosser's evidence got most – but not all – of them put away." Erica chuckled softly. "He was pleased he didn't have to deal with Prosser again, don't think he liked him very much."

"That is good news, that loose end really got under my skin. Does Dilys know she was right?"

"I'll speak to her first thing on Tuesday, and there is just a little more..."

"What else could there be?" Matt asked.

"Lois Clarke was laundering money through her company for her scummy, scammer brother. She has been charged and will go to court at the end of the summer. I predict plenty of prison time, given the circumstances and the amounts of money involved."

Fabia raised her brandy glass. "I've got a toast," she said. "To the good guys."

* * *

A while later, as the afternoon drew to a close and the evening began, Erica got to her feet.

"Such a wonderful lunch," she said. "Many thanks."

"My pleasure," Fabia said. "Let me get your coat and show you out."

At the front door, Erica turned to look at her host.

"The LSCB meeting on Tuesday has been cancelled again, I'm afraid."

"Not again!" said Fabia. "Chairing those awful meetings isn't what I thought it would be. Half of them can't even be bothered to turn up."

"Which works to our advantage."

"Does it?"

Erica nodded. "Your talents are being wasted there, which is why I want to see you in my office on Tuesday at

10.30. It's time you and I have a serious discussion about your future with the force. I want you on my team, and I'm good at getting what I want." She gave Fabia a very quick hug. "Thank you again for the wonderful meal. I'll see you on Tuesday."

Fabia watched as Erica got in her car and pulled away from the house. She remained on the step, gazing towards the mountains, half-hidden by the twilight, and took a deep breath of the cool fresh air. Then she straightened her shoulders and headed to the living room to tell Matt the exciting news.

THE END

# Character list

Fabia Havard – artist and ex-police superintendent, Matt Lambert's partner

Bethan Havard – Fabia and Matt's nine-month-old daughter

Cath Temple – Vicar of St Cybi's Church and close friend of Fabia

Aled Jameson

Cai Roberts – Aled's cousin

Chelsea Jameson – Aled's mother

Huw Prosser – parishioner and sidesman at St Cybi's Church

Jake Seddon – pharmacist from Bridgend

Gwyneth Seddon – Jake's wife

Dai & Paul Michaelson – local criminals and Gwyneth Seddon's cousins

Cari Michaelson – Dai & Paul's mother

Mr Cheng – owner of Lotus Flower restaurant/takeaway in Usk

Seth Geddings – scammer and Mr Cheng's tenant

Lois Clarke – Seth's sister

Alys Penry – one of Seth Geddings' victims

Ena Williams – Huw Prosser's neighbour

Gareth Daniels – a journalist and podcaster, Chloe Daniels' brother

Keith Prendergast – author working in Gareth's office, friend of his editor

*Police personnel:*

Detective Chief Inspector Matt Lambert of Newport Police – Fabia's partner

Detective Sergeant Dilys Bevan

Chief Superintendent Erica Talbot – Matt's boss

Inspector Ashok Kapoor of the South Wales force, Bridgend

Police Constable Chloe Daniels

Police Constable Craig Evans

Detective Constable Tom Watkins

Detective Constable Sara Gupta

Detective Constable Becca Pryce

Police Constable Karim Singh

Police Constable Aidan Rogers – IT expert

Karen Johns – crime scene supervisor

Dr Pat Curtis – police surgeon

Detective Sergeant Gwyn Jones – retired officer

Detective Inspector Glyn Evans

## Publisher's note and acknowledgements

Pippa was a wonderful writer and a kind and generous person, who dedicated her life to helping others. Having lived in Swansea for many years, Wales was very close to her heart. And with its majestic countryside and communities of colourful characters, it was an obvious place to set her mystery fiction. Her passing is a great loss to the literary world, but will of course be felt most sorely by her family and friends.

We would like to thank Pippa's husband, Niall, and her sons, James, Toby and Sam, for assisting us with bringing out this work posthumously. We hope we have done justice to the high standards Pippa expected of herself. Thanks also to Pippa's dear friend, Jeannie Palmer, who provided invaluable insight and advice.

Many thanks too, to author Nicola Clifford, who took on the unenviable task of completing this unfinished work. Nicola's own writing shares many of the qualities of Pippa's – a strong love for Wales and its people, and a deep concern for social justice – so she was well positioned to take on the task, and handled it with skill and delicacy.

If you enjoyed this book, please let others know by leaving a quick review on Amazon. Also, if you spot anything untoward in the paperback, get in touch. We strive for the best quality and appreciate reader feedback.

editor@thebookfolks.com

www.thebookfolks.com

**Also by Pippa McCathie:**

MURDER IN THE VALLEYS

*The first book to feature Fabia Havard and Matt Lambert*

Having left the police following a corruption investigation, ex-superintendent Fabia Havard is struggling with civilian life. When a girl is murdered in her town, she can't help trying to find the killer. Will her former colleague Matt Lambert stop her, or realize the value of his former boss to the floundering inquiry?

*Available in paperback, audio, and FREE with Kindle Unlimited.*

MURDER AT THE OLD ABBEY

*The second book to feature Fabia Havard and Matt Lambert*

When an overbearing patriarch and much begrudged ex-army officer is found dead in his home, there is no shortage of suspects. DCI Matt Lambert investigates, but struggles with a lack of evidence. He'll have to rely on his former boss, ex-detective Fabia Havard, to help him. But will their fractious relationship get in the way of solving the case?

*Available in paperback, audio, and FREE with Kindle Unlimited.*

MURDER BY THE RIVER USK

*The third book to feature Fabia Havard and Matt Lambert*

Almost ten years after he went missing, a student's body is found. Forensics show that he was murdered and a cold case is reopened. But when detectives begin to investigate his background, many people he knew are found to be keeping a secret of sorts. Faced with subterfuge and deceit, rooting out the true killer will take all their detective skills.

*Available in paperback, audio, and FREE with Kindle Unlimited.*

MURDER IN A WELSH TOWN

*The fourth book to feature Fabia Havard and Matt Lambert*

Hopes for a town pantomime are dashed when a participant is found murdered. The victim was the town gossip and there is no shortage of people who had a grudge to bear against him. Detective Matt Lambert leads the investigation but draws on the help of his girlfriend, ex-police officer Fabia Havard. Can they solve the crime together?

*Available in paperback, audio, and FREE with Kindle Unlimited.*

LIBERATION DAY

*A standalone romantic thriller*

Having become stranded in the English Channel after commandeering her cheating boyfriend's boat, Caro is rescued by a handsome stranger. But when the boat is impounded on suspicion of smuggling, she once again finds herself in deep water.

*Available in paperback and FREE with Kindle Unlimited.*

THE ISLAND BRIEF

*A stirring romantic suspense*

When Abi receives a surprise letter about an inheritance, it brings memories of her childhood on the island of Mauritius flooding back. Plus, a recollection of the sender, Raj, now a lawyer but then a small boy who was on the receiving end of her childish pranks. She feels the desire to return, but is it just the island drawing her back?

*Available in paperback and FREE with Kindle Unlimited.*

**Other titles of interest:**

NO REFUGE by Nicola Clifford

Reporter Stacey Logan has little to worry about other than the town flower festival when a man is shot dead. When she believes the police have got the wrong man, she does some snooping of her own. But will her desire for a scoop lead her to a place where there is no refuge?

*Available in paperback and FREE with Kindle Unlimited.*

THE SILENT QUARRY by Cheryl Rees-Price

Following a fall and a bang to the head, a woman's memories come flooding back about an incident that occurred twenty years ago in which her friend was murdered. As she pieces together the events and tells the police, she begins to fear repercussions. DI Winter Meadows must work out the identity of the killer before they strike again.

*Available in paperback and FREE with Kindle Unlimited.*

THE
BOOK
FOLKS

Printed in Great Britain
by Amazon

52656046R00142